HIS PLEDGE TO HOLD

A SILVER STAR RANCH ROMANCE

SHANAE JOHNSON

CHAPTER ONE

Truman Bates sunk into the quiet of his surroundings. Even the insects seemed to hush as he lay his form against the cool earth. The four-legged mammals made no sound either. The metal resting against his shoulder proved that he was the biggest, baddest predator out in these woods today.

There were no claws at the ends of his sure hands. No deadly antlers protruded from the cap covering his dark hair. He was even clean-shaven, not possessing the funk that would ward off any oncoming foe. It was the metal behemoth that kept all others at bay.

However, Truman's finger was not on the trigger of his rifle. It was on the microscopic lens that doubled as his eyes. He rotated the scope using the grooves on the wheel. All of his focus was on his target. The exercise right now was training his eyes to find the details in plain sight of the scope.

With his vision magnified, Truman could see the details that even an owl couldn't pick up. The turn of the blade of grass in the light breeze. The fall of a leaf as its weight got too heavy for the tree limb. The movement of a pebble as an insect carved a path in new growth.

Nature continued its business in quiet activity. This was how Truman had learned most of his training as a sniper for the US Military. Snipers were masters of hiding in plain sight. They excelled at watching over, or even under, both a target they aimed to take out as well as the person whose back they were tasked with protecting. A sniper's ability to become one with their environment trained them to spot enemies and to take out threats without being detected by man, beast, or even owl.

There were no owls high up in trees today. No snakes slithering through the grasses. Only a bull's eye placed a thousand meters away. It was a little over half a mile. On his best day, he had managed twelve hundred meters. He was hoping his better days were ahead of him. For now, he needed to remaster this distance.

With his eye in the scope, Truman fingered the trigger. When he was ready, he pulled his index finger back. The zip of the bullet whizzing through the air hit his ears as the kickback of the gun hit his shoulder.

Truman grunted, tamping down as much of the pain as he could. It still hurt. The injury may have shouted, but so did the target. Truman had managed to hit the bull's eye.

He couldn't hear the thud of the impact. But he could see it. A perfect black hole in the center of the yellow paper.

Silence was all that cheered on his victory. Until Truman let out a low sigh that turned to a groan. The groan became a grunt as he rolled onto his back.

Now that the tension was released, all he could feel was the recoil that had hit his injured shoulder. Truman's calculations had been perfect. He'd accounted for everything but that.

There was nothing wrong with his aim. The only problem rested tirelessly in his shoulder, where he could no longer lift his rifle without pain. Right now, the ground was taking on the weight of his weapon. Unfortunately, the job of a sniper didn't always call for him to lie in wait with a surface under him to take the weight of his weapon. If he couldn't lift the rifle in protection of anyone in his unit, then he was as good as dead. Which was how he felt at the moment while his shoulder throbbed from the blow the rifle had dealt it.

Instead of letting the rifle go, Truman clung to it. For so many years, it had been his constant companion. Never letting him down until that fateful day when he could no longer carry it.

The sound of gunfire. Of his brothers' shouts. Of women screaming. Of the blast that stole the general's last command. Those sounds played in repeat inside Truman's once-quiet head. So, when the sounds of twigs breaking and footsteps approaching reached him in the present moment, it was too late for him to react.

Someone was coming. It was clear to hear that that someone wasn't a soldier. Each of the President's Men knew he was shooting out here. They knew he was trying to recapture his precision, his strength. They knew he didn't want company as he tried to dig himself out of this particular hole.

Because they all knew that, they would announce their presence by calling out to him. Which meant that whoever was coming wasn't one of his fellow soldiers. Whoever was coming was coming in hot.

Truman reached for his weapon. He rolled to his side, wrapping his arms around it. Then he rolled onto his back with the rifle in tow.

Too bad his grunt of pain was just as loud as the encroaching enemy. Truman grimaced as his shoulder protested the weight of the gun. It mutinied when he ordered the muscles to arrange themselves in the position he needed to hold the weapon in order to defend himself. He managed to rest the stock of the rifle against the ground, giving him leverage to get in position when a form came out of the bushes.

Wild blonde hair flew into view. Followed by blue eyes blazing so bright, they were all that would be seen before the storm swept in.

It was Tilly. What was she doing out here? Shouldn't she be holed up with Carter, her new hubby?

But no, this wasn't Tilly. Tilly wore pretty sundresses and makeup. Which was why she was perfect for Truman's best friend, who was fastidious when it came to his dress and appearance.

This Tilly imposter wore ill-fitting cargo pants, combat boots, and a rainbow t-shirt with animals frolicking underneath the rays. There wasn't an ounce of makeup to mask her irate features.

"Gunnery?" Truman asked, naming Tilly's twin sister.

In answer, Gunnery kicked the rifle out of his hand. Had his shoulder been what it was, the move would've never worked. But as it was, the gun clattered out of his hands and onto the ground as he muttered a curse of discomfort and incredulity.

Truman had just been ungunned by a slip of a girl. Well, she was a Silver. The daughter of a general who took no prisoners. So he could always claim that as his excuse if the rest of the guys, or even her older sister Scout, ever found out.

"What do you think you're doing?" Gunny hissed.

CHAPTER TWO

*S*o, she was back home. Second time in less than a year. It was a record.

Gunnery Silver tilted her head back and looked out at the splendor of the Silver Star Ranch. All she could see was green. A green so lush it looked like it could be a mirage. Just a few days ago, she would've sworn it was.

Just last week, she'd been in the Namib Desert. Tracking and studying the Namib Desert Horse. The creature was native to the African continent, but only by way of transplant. Likely thanks to German cavalry horses.

Not only were the horses a magnificent athletic specimen, they had evolved to withstand the harsh desert climate. Most of the time, they thrived in the harsh, barren conditions. Unless there was famine. Or drought. Or worse, human interference.

It never ceased to amaze Gunny how much damage humankind did to this planet. Mankind roamed around bulldozing, flattening the lands as if they truly owned the entire Earth. But no one could ever own land, not truly. Not even when they produced a scrap of paper with some ink on it. Because they had to wait for that same scrap of parchment to sprout from the earth just to claim the land.

It was idiotic.

Still, no matter how much she shouted, most people didn't care to listen to her. But Gunny still railed at the top of her lungs. She had to. The animals, the environment, neither had a voice of their own. If she didn't fight with all her might, more lands would turn to waste, more animals would become endangered.

Some fights she won. Some fights... well, she wouldn't say she'd lost. She just moved on to another battle and would come back another day. A fight was never over until she had won it.

The Silver Star ranch was the only place she didn't have to fight. There was no danger of her home turning into a human wasteland where trees withered and animals disappeared. The place was as vibrant as the day Gunny had learned to walk on the land. From every corner, the ranch teemed with life. The funny thing was, she was the endangered species on the property.

Gunny was the last single Silver daughter. All five of her sisters were married. Except her. And if she didn't get married soon, they would lose this haven for flora and fauna.

It was almost contradictory. Because as she'd said, Gunny didn't believe that land was owned, not truly. But she did know that if her wicked stepmother got her hands on this land, then Catherine would definitely raze it to the ground. Not a green shrub would remain after Cruella flew by on her broom. Not a horse would have a place to eat its hay. Not a bunny would have a hole to hide in.

Her beliefs aside, Gunny couldn't let that happen. So, she'd get married. And then she'd be out of here.

She just had to wait for her sisters to figure out which soldier she was supposed to marry. Already the two men that had been earmarked for her had been swiped up by her sisters. So much for their lessons in sibling sharing.

But one look at her baby sister Brig with her hubby Jackson, and Gunny knew the two were meant to spend the rest of their days together. Only a slightly older man could handle the maturity that Brig and her intelligence brought to the table.

Gunny had had her doubts about her twin's beau, Carter. But when she'd witnessed the devastation in the man's eyes that he'd potentially lost Tilly, Gunny knew the man was hopelessly in love and would move heaven and earth to get Tilly back and keep her. Plus, he was far too groomed for Gunny's tastes.

She needed a man who liked the outdoors. A man who didn't mind a little dirt under his fingernails. A man who loved animals and wanted to preserve the Earth as much as she did.

There was one soldier left. She had yet to meet Truman Bates. She doubted the man would live up to her list. But he didn't need to. She just needed to marry him to get the deed, and then she was out of here. It didn't matter if he had a preservation consciousness or not.

A crack split the air. Followed by a whizzing hiss. Then the sound of a thud as the impact was made.

Gunny froze. She knew that sound. It was unmistakable. But what was it doing here in her backyard?

Using the senses and skills she'd learned from her general of a father, Gunny zeroed in on the location. She could see a bull's eye in the distance, but not the shooter. Someone was shooting on her land.

It had to be one of the soldiers. How dare he? She would give her new brother-in-law an earful about hunting on this land that was purposed solely for horse rehab and not for killing any living soul.

But that would only be if she could find the man. She saw the bull's eye, but she didn't see any human tracks. He couldn't be far. No one could shoot more than a thousand meters and hit a bull's eye.

Gunny was starting to wonder if she had been hearing things when she nearly stumbled over the body. When she looked down, she saw the face of a stranger. He wasn't one of the five new brothers-in-law that she had met. He didn't seem brotherly at all, not with the rifle trained on her.

Indignation got the better of her. Gunny kicked the gun out of his hands with her boot. Surprisingly, it fell out of his hold. Then, even more surprisingly than the gunman letting loose his weapon, he hissed in pain.

She had no idea why? Her boot hadn't made contact with his skin—yet. She'd only kicked the weapon.

Slowly, the gunman's gaze narrowed on her in recognition. "Gunnery?" he asked.

"What do you think you're doing?" she hissed. "There's no shooting on this land. You might've hurt something."

"Something?" he said, rolling to his haunches. "There are no people or animals out here. And if there were, I wouldn't shoot them."

"You can't control a bullet."

"I can if it's coming from my weapon." The man stood up. And up. And then he straightened to stand a bit more up.

He was tall. Tall enough to rival the trees surrounding them. Tall enough to block out the sun.

Gunny gave herself a shake to focus on the matter at hand. The man had been shooting on her family ranch. No one from town would have the audacity.

"Let me guess," she said. "You're the sixth soldier from my father's unit?"

"Truman Bates, sniper of the President's Men, at your service."

He didn't hold out a hand for her to shake. It was still gripping his shoulder. Gunny wouldn't have taken his hand if he had offered it to her. Not in greeting. Not in matrimony.

"No," she said.

"No, what?"

"No, this is not going to happen." She waved her hand, motioning between them. But he wasn't looking at her. He was reaching for his weapon. Not with his right hand, which had been the shoulder he'd been holding. He reached with his left hand. The move was awkward, as though he were right-handed by nature and was picking up a pencil with his left.

"Look," he said, once the weapon was clutched in his left hand. "Scout said it was fine if I shoot as long as I come all the way out here."

Did Scout really think Gunny would marry a sniper? "Well, Scout was wrong."

"Are you calling me a liar?"

"I'm not calling you anything. Especially not husband."

Truman blanched as he looked at her. And suddenly, Gunny wondered if she had it all wrong. Her sisters would've known she would never marry a gunman. Not to save her family, not to save all the animals and land in the world. There simply was no way.

And then Truman the Sniper opened his mouth and confirmed the facts as they stood. "I have no plans to marry you."

CHAPTER THREE

ruman looked between his gun and Gunnery. In another life, he may have gotten a kick out of that. A woman named after his favorite pastime in the world. The term gunnery meant the use of guns. But as Gunnery Silver sneered down at Truman's most prized possession, his gun, he got the distinct impression that she wasn't a fan of either of them.

Her round pink lips were curled down at one end, flashing a hint of sharp incisors. Her heart-shaped nose was wrinkled, as though she smelled something foul. That slender swan's neck of hers undulated as though she were finding it hard to swallow something. That was not the look of a woman who enjoyed shooting.

"I have no plan to marry you," he said.

And he didn't. True, he had no plan to marry anyone. Definitely not a woman who was clearly his exact opposite.

Gunny Silver looked like a tiny warrior standing over him. But the worst kind of warrior. She believed that peace came at no cost. She was wrong. Truman knew the price of peace firsthand as someone with personal knowledge of the balance sheet of the ledger.

"At least that we can agree on," she said.

She crossed her arms over her chest. Truman's eyes were drawn there, and he immediately looked away. Not because he didn't want to be caught staring at her chest. More because the sight hurt his eyes.

For such a tiny woman, Gunny was loud. Not just in her voice but in her clothing as well. She wore green camouflaged pants that only came to her mid-calf. There was a patch of toned leg exposed before the eye reached her hiking boots.

The camo pants were all well and good out in nature. What Truman couldn't understand was why she would couple them with a bright pink shirt that read *Be Kind to Every Kind*. Green was everywhere and could hide her. But there was no shade of pink like that in nature, not unless nature was a drugstore full of Pepto Bismol.

"I could never bring myself to let a man with gunpowder on his hands touch me," she said.

"Now, now," Truman tsked. "That doesn't sound very kind to one of my kind."

He pointed at her shirt. When she looked down to follow the trajectory of his index finger, it looked as though he was pointing at her breast. Truman retracted his finger.

"I don't think killing is very kind," she said, those blue eyes shooting fire at him.

Little did Gunny know that blue was the hottest part of the flame. Or maybe she did know that, and that's why she was shooting those sparks at him with her eyes. What she didn't realize was that it was making Truman warm all up and down his limbs.

He needed to shake this insane feeling. The woman had just called him a killer. And she wasn't wrong.

The military had trained him to take out bad guys swiftly, efficiently, and quietly. Those were his best and brightest skills. His only skills. If he didn't regain his proficiency—and soon—he had no idea what he'd do with the rest of his life.

He knew for certain that he wasn't going to

marry this Silver woman. He had no intention of following the path of the other President's Men. He was still a fighter.

So why did his heart kick against his chest at the thought of not marrying Gunny Silver? Why did his blood elevate at the thought of another man taking on that job?

She was not his type.

Not in any way.

First off, she was a civilian. Truman had only ever dated women in the service. They knew the score. They didn't question his job. Or his absences. Or the bloodstains that wouldn't come out of his shirts.

Secondly, Gunny stood against everything that he crept through hostile environments to defend. Truman had no qualms with the rights of animals. So long as they were served on his plate or kept in the backyard. Environmental protection was a concern of his, but only when it came to guarding the borders of his country and the boundaries of his homestead. And peace? Well, peace was the ultimate goal.

Third—and by far the most important reason that Gunny Silver was not for him—was that she required a ring. Truman was a young, virile man, even with his injury. He had dated much and looked forward to getting back on that saddle. But he planned never to be saddled with a wife, not with his line of work.

And so, with that, he took a deep breath into his chest. With an exhale, his blood settled back to its normal temperature. He pulled his weapon to his chest, preparing to get away from this vociferously dressed and roaringly opinionated woman. But as the full weight of the gun came up against his shoulder, he winced and stumbled backward.

"Are you hurt?" Gunny asked. The pinch in her brow gone. What was left was a smooth line of concern as she reached out to him.

The sweet scent of cloves filled his nose. The strong earthy scent reminded him of his mother rubbing Tiger Balm on his chest when he had a cold. Truman had continued the use of the topical cream whenever he had any aches and pains. It was also an insect repellant for when he was in the field.

For a moment, all of the pain in his shoulder went away. Along with his cares about getting cleared. All that mattered was the scent and sensation of the woman at his side.

With his mind so preoccupied with the peace she brought, Truman failed to react when Gunny took his gun from his hand. Never before had anyone, friend or foe, managed to disarm him. But this protesting, prismatic, pint-sized woman managed to with little resistance.

"I'm fine," Truman said, reaching for his weapon. Only, his hand didn't make it very far. Because his eyes liked what he was seeing.

Gunny was looking his rifle up and down. Truman felt as though she was examining him as a man, measuring his worth and value in the weapon he used to defend himself and make his livelihood. She'd been holding the rifle sideways in her inspection. Now, she turned it upright, tucking it against her side.

She didn't aim it at him. She aimed it at the ground. And then, with practiced fingers that moved as though the digits had done this a thousand times, she flicked her thumb over the selector switch, ensuring the weapon wouldn't discharge automatically or accidentally.

Truman watched her. He should've been livid that she held his gun. Or at least ill at ease. But once again, his heart was kicking inside his chest. Harder this time, as though it wanted out of its cage. His blood was scalding hot in his veins, as though it knew the blue of her eyes was the only thing that would cool the heat.

Truman stood staring at Gunnery Silver with her bright camouflage that would never hide her. And he liked the look of her with his weapon in her hands.

CHAPTER FOUR

The feel of the cool steel in her hand made Gunny's chest feel hollow. Her palms dampened, and she worried the weapon might fall from her hands. The next thing she knew, the rifle was removed from her hold.

Gunny looked up into eyes, the same cool steel color of the death machine. She saw loss in those gray eyes. She saw pain and torment.

Instead of feeling that this soldier had got his due, Gunny felt the sudden urge to wrap her arms around Truman and rub up and down his back. Just like her second mom Sarah had done for her anytime Gunny had awakened in the night with phantom memories of the birth mother Gunny hadn't gotten the chance to know.

Roxanne Silver's eyes had been gray. Gunny knew because she'd seen pictures. Her birth mother had been beautiful, though frail. She'd never understood why her father, a strong and commanding general, had picked Roxanne. But Gunny was grateful because her father's choice had brought her Sarah and all of her sisters.

Now her sisters would lose everything if Gunny didn't follow her father's outrageous demands and find a husband before the end of the week. Looking at this man with gun metal eyes, Gunny could see the appeal another woman would find in him.

Along with those arresting eyes, Truman Bates had a strong square jaw. There was even a dimple right, smack dab at the center of his chin that Kurt Russell would've envied. A five o'clock shadow darkened his cheeks. A few tendrils of dark hair escaped his camouflage-colored cap.

Truman was a handsome man. By the looks of him, he was a capable man. If only he didn't cradle that rifle like it was his long-lost lover. That was so not cute.

He'd said he was fine when clearly his shoulder was sore. Gunny had caught the grimace when she'd kicked the gun. She caught it again when he retrieved his weapon from her with his right hand.

He was injured, but just like a man, he wasn't owning up to it.

"Of course you'd say you're fine," she said. "Pain is fear leaving the body, right? My dad used to say that all the time."

"My mother said it, too."

A grin lit up his features. That steel gray felt like a ray of sunshine at the mention of his mother. His smile looked soft and welcoming, like a pillow Gunny wanted to rest against her forehead, against her nose, against her mouth.

"She was in the Army," he continued. "One of the first female snipers."

Gunny was hard-wired to form a bad opinion of anyone with a gun. She preferred to use her words to solve the world's problems, not weapons. She'd start with trying to have a civil conversation. When that didn't work, she began to shout. When that didn't work, she picked up a pen. Instead of pouring ink down her adversaries' throats, which she often daydreamed of doing, she penned letters instead. Letters of protests. Letters to legislators. Letters to conservation and humanitarian organizations.

"I'm not sure how to feel about that," Gunny said. "One part of me wants to cheer for her addition to the cause of women's advancement in the workplace."

Truman's bright grin turned to a smirk. The way he parted his lips made Gunny's brain stutter for a second. She gave herself a shake and found more words to hurl at him.

"But those same cheers she deserves for breaking down one barrier are clashing with my activism side for gun control."

"She was killed in the line of duty by a thirteen-year-old child soldier. The gun he carried was bigger than he was."

"I… I'm sorry."

He blinked, as though coming back to the present. That steely gray gaze focused on her. His eyes roamed her face, searching for… she didn't know what he was hoping to find. But she held still for him.

"She took him out before she succumbed to her injuries." His voice sounded hollow as he spoke. "The kid and I were the same age, and she had to shoot him so he couldn't hurt anybody else."

Gunny did reach for him then. Her hand landed on his shoulder cap. His right shoulder cap where she knew he was hiding even more pain.

Truman pulled away from her touch. He sat

down, pulling the rifle onto his lap, and began disassembling the weapon. His fingers were fast and sure, as though he'd done this a thousand times. Because he likely had.

"This is why I'm for gun control," she said. "A bullet doesn't just hurt the one it's aimed at, it hurts entire families and societies for generations."

It was the wrong thing to say after he bared his pain. She knew that. She knew it as she was saying it. But it was a truth she believed so wholeheartedly that she didn't think twice.

"Ever notice how bad guys don't follow the laws," he said. "It's kind of their thing."

"If world governments made it harder for the bad guys to get their hands on weapons, then it wouldn't be their thing."

Truman stood up. And up. And up.

He'd only been sitting for a few moments, but in that time Gunny had forgotten how tall he was. Now that she was so close to him, she saw how broad he was as well. He blocked out the sun. The only source of illumination were those silver-gray eyes. And they were cloudy as they narrowed on her.

Gunny braced herself for battle. Though something in her quaked and shook loose. She had a feeling that Truman Bates would be a worthy opponent. She'd have to bring her A-game. Likely her B and C game as well.

Except then he pulled a move she didn't see coming from miles away. He pulled her to him, wrapping his arms around her body and tucking her head into his chest.

The quaking and shaking made its way up from the heel of her boots. It grew until her knees knocked together. Her heart rate didn't increase, but she felt the thumps like fists against her rib cage.

What was happening to her?

"Don't worry. I've got you."

It was the sound of Truman's deep voice that brought her back to her senses. It was the ground that was shaking, not her. That kind of rumbling could only come from one place. Gunny lifted her head and saw confirmation.

Off in the distance, she saw a herd of wild mustangs running across the land. Black-coated stallions. Majestic brown steeds. White-haired beauties. They ran as a group, kicking up dust in their wake.

All Gunny could do was stand there and watch as they raced by, free as the day they were born. She could hear the rhythm of life beating strong as she lay her ear against a strong chest.

Wait! What? Her ear was against Truman's chest. She was still wrapped up in Truman's embrace as they both watched the scene play out before them.

He must have thought they were in danger from the horses. Though it was never wise to approach a wild horse, they preferred to avoid humans. And besides, it was Gunny who had fought for their freedom years ago.

Since she was in no danger from the animals, there was no reason for her to be in this soldier's embrace. She lifted her head and immediately missed the musicality of his heartbeat. She took a step back and instantly missed the heat from his body.

When gray eyes met blue, she felt lost in a land she knew like the back of her hand. She cleared her throat once, twice. Finally, she was able to get out the only words that mattered.

"I'm not going to marry you," she said.

Truman swallowed a few times. His Adam's apple bobbing as though it was having trouble getting words past his throat. "I'm not going to marry you, either."

"Glad that's settled."

"Me, too."

They stood staring at each other. The horses were long gone, but their dust was still floating in the air. It felt like tumbleweeds had rolled through in a western stand-off.

The gun was a dividing line between them on the ground. Her sisters thought she would marry this man? Not if he was the last man on earth. Luckily, he wasn't.

"Well," she said, "have a nice life, Truman Bates."

"Same to you, Gunnery Silver."

Gunny turned her back on him. She'd come out here for a reason. In the distance, she could see the Flying Cross Ranch. There were six perfectly good specimens of men who'd grown up next door. Surely one of them would help an old friend out to save Silver Star.

CHAPTER FIVE

Truman turned the knob to head inside his cabin. Technically, it was Scout's cabin. Before moving in here a few weeks ago, he'd been staying in Brig's cabin. But once she and Jackson tied the knot, he gave them that space.

Scout's cabin was spartan and utilitarian. Much like the woman who had built it. It suited Truman's needs just fine, as he didn't have many belongings and didn't require that much space. The life of a sniper demanded few attachments.

Truman clenched his fist and then shook out his fingers. Unfortunately, the move didn't mute the feel of having a woman in his arms for the first time in… he couldn't even remember how long it had been since he'd last held a woman. He knew not one single time could compare to pressing Gunny Silver's curves against his form.

He'd been surprised to find supple arcs and contours inside those two contradicting fabrics she wore. Gunny was built nothing like her namesake. Truman's trigger finger itched to bend her form to him once more.

But they'd already agreed. Neither wanted to marry the other. Though Truman was seriously shaky on his pronouncement.

He knew it wasn't meant to be. He was headed back to the military. She was headed to the Flying Cross Ranch to make a deal with one of Father Matthews' sons.

Truman wasn't even aware that any of the old man's boys were at home. He'd never met a single one of them in the months he'd been living at Silver Star Ranch. So why did he have the urge to punch out any one of them who might take Gunny up on her offer of a convenient marriage?

Truman didn't like the woman. He couldn't even stand being in her cabin. He'd taken one look in Gunny's cabin two and a half months ago and backpedaled it out of there like a cartoon character. PETA posters had been plastered over the walls.

Along with *Save the Whales* and *Let Wild Horses Roam Free.*

It wasn't that Truman disagreed with any of those sentiments. He preferred to do his hunting in grocery stores like a normal twenty-first-century man. Guns were for protection, not sport. What his country needed to be protected from most were terrorists and extremists. Which meant his attentions, and the barrel of his gun, were aimed at bad humans and not animals.

He was certain he could never explain his views to Gunny Silver. She probably thought the United States Military should work out their problems with Jihadists while holding hands and singing *Kumbaya.*

So, nope, the two of them would never suit. Not even if the feel of her breath against his neck had sparked a fire in him that was still messing with his head. He went to the small fridge and pulled out a cold beer. Instead of drinking it, he pressed it to his forehead.

It wasn't that Truman had never thought of marriage and a family. He had. For his friends. Not for him. He would be happy being Uncle Truman, teaching the little girls to shoot and the young boys how to hide in plain sight.

But a wife of his own? That was impractical

since he planned to spend all of his days fighting alongside his brothers and sisters in the military. His family would never see him. That method worked great for his role as a sniper, but not for a wife and kids.

Truman heard voices outside. He sat his unopened beer down and went to the window. Linc and Jefferson rode horses side by side. They brought the horses to a stop and chatted to each other.

As always, neither man could see him. Truman had always been in the shadows as he had their backs. But he'd failed them on that last mission.

It didn't seem like any of them cared. They weren't concerned about their backs any longer. Not when they each looked forward to a future with their wives.

The war was over for them. This, this ranch, these Silver girls, this was their reward.

A knock came at his door. Before Truman made his way over to open it, Linc strode in.

"This came for you," Linc said.

The envelope in his hands was from the latest recruiter Truman had been working with. Though all of his unit had been medically discharged due to their injuries, Truman wanted back in active duty.

He craved the action, needed the responsibility. But he needed a waiver to do so.

For the past year, Truman had been told that the type of waiver he'd need would require a shipload of paperwork. The person who'd told him that hadn't exaggerated enough. The paperwork had been mountainous. The work wasn't for the faint of heart. Truman had gone through two other recruiters who'd given up on the insurmountable task in a matter of weeks. Until he'd found one who'd stuck it out with him.

This latest recruiter had streamlined the paperwork and gave Truman hope. Truman was told he simply needed to find a surgeon who would clear him for duty. A feat which was easier said than done.

Truman had been to surgeon after surgeon in the last four months. Each one had expressed doubt over his ability to perform his duties. Until Dr. Hunter.

True, the man had been practicing in Cancun. And the degree on the wall looked as though there was a smudge of white-out on the document. But Dr. Hunter had told Truman what he'd wanted to hear. Beyond that, the good doctor had written a report to the recruiter.

In that envelope was the military's final decision. Truman reached for it. He winced at the dull pain in his shoulder as he did so. That didn't deter him from tearing the thin document out.

And then the small pain in his arm was forgotten. His heart dropped to the floor after the first line.

Denied.

Limitation in motion.

No appeals.

It was over. Truman wasn't sure what crumpled to the ground first? Him or the letter.

"There's always contract work," said Linc, who had sat down beside him.

Truman wasn't sure how long they had sat there? Maybe a few minutes? Maybe an hour?

Truman looked up at his friend. Linc was always ready with a plan. The problem was contract work wasn't in Truman's plan. Those men were often more loyal to a paycheck than their country.

"Or, there's the original backup plan," said Linc. "You marry into this family."

Truman opened his mouth to speak, to tell Linc that it would never work between him and Gunny. Truman wasn't sure if his mouth shut before it could lie or if Linc cut him off.

"It would be the only marriage of convenience, which there's no law against. You two wouldn't have to see each other after the ceremony. She'll be going back overseas. You'll be looking into contract work. But it'll keep us all intact. It'll give you both a home you can always come back to."

That's what did it. Truman couldn't break his team up. At least this way, he would have their backs one last time.

CHAPTER SIX

Gunny took the long way round to the Flying Cross Ranch. She needed the walk in nature to cool her temper. Her boots left the wildflowers her stepmother Sarah had sprinkled in every corner of the ranch, only to crunch over dry, caked earth that had been left unattended for years as she drew nearer to the edge of the property line.

The nerve of that man. Had Truman really questioned her intelligence? Of course, she knew that bad guys didn't follow laws. But sometimes, it was the bad guys that made the laws.

Gunny snapped her fingers. That's what she should have said to him as a comeback. She had half a mind to turn around, march back up to him, and deliver the line.

Only she knew he was long gone. Packed up his killing machine and gone back to his cabin. Belatedly, she wondered whose cabin he was sleeping in?

The thought of Truman Bates curled up in her eco-friendly, zero waste, organic eucalyptus sheets made her blood heat. Not in an angry way. In the way where she had to lift both her hands and fan her face.

What was wrong with her? She couldn't be attracted to him. His coworker was a rifle. The man had a body count for crying out loud.

He was a gun-toting, war-loving fascist. Or worst, capitalist. She had no problem with communism and socialism. The roots of the words implied family. Though her sisters had miscalculated if they thought she would've ever considered Truman the Sniper for a real marriage or even a sham one.

Which was why Gunny would have to take matters into her own hands.

At the edge of the Flying Cross Ranch property line, Gunny saw movement. It was a movement of the four-legged kind. But these two animals weren't large enough for her to mount. Two deer roamed just beyond the fenced boundary; a mom and her fawn.

Gunny stood and watched the pair. Even though the film *Bambi* had traumatized her at a young age. Scout should've never shown that film to a child who had lost her mother shortly after she'd been born. Gunny was certain that movie had imprinted on her and pointed her on her life's mission to save all the world's animals from hunters' guns.

All over the world, mankind was ravaging forests, jungles, and valleys that were once sacred to all kinds of flora and fauna. Hunters killed for sport, not for sustenance. The never-thinning human herd was laying waste to much of the world's natural resources and life forms. Gunny was resolved to put a stop to it.

She had lost two mothers, but she would not lose her home. Which was why Gunny needed to protect this land. She might not want to stand still on the Silver Star Ranch, but this was where her roots were planted. She wasn't going to let anyone take this away from her family.

Marrying that gun-happy soldier was a bridge too far. Truman could've shot and killed Bambi himself. He'd been close to taking out one of the wild horses that ran freely through all these lands.

He had been a good shot. Seeing as the only thing he aimed at was the target, and he'd hit it. Still, he was far from her type.

Gunny wasn't exactly sure she had a type. The few men who joined her in her crusades were either old hippies with gray hair and poor hygiene. Or they were young hipsters with top knots and floral-scented soaps. She couldn't take a man with a pony-tail seriously.

No, Gunny had a better idea. Which was why she marched onto the land of the Flying Cross Ranch. She still couldn't fathom why her sisters had married those strangers when there had been six Matthews boys next door. The Silver sisters had always been able to get the Matthews boys to do what they wanted. Now, in their time of absolute need, should be no different.

As Gunny made her way up the drive, she saw a familiar vehicle in the driveway next to Father Matthews's beat-up, old truck. The other vehicle was a minivan that had seen better days. But those days had to have happened long before Gunny had been born because the vehicle was at least twice her age. Bright Horizons Foster Care was painted on the side. The yellow paint of the sun's rays was chipped. And it looked as though someone had spray-painted a gray swirl of smoke from the smiling sun's lips to make it look as though the star was having a cigarette. Or at least Gunny hoped that was meant to be a cigarette.

Climbing the stairs, she heard a familiar voice coming from within the house. The voice was deep and raspy, making the owner sound like she was a longtime smoker. Gunny had heard that voice sing the most soulful tunes before.

"The city is saying the federal government is taking the land. Which means they're going to demolish the foster home, and we'll all be kicked out."

Savy James stood with her hands on generous hips. Even in a pair of worn jeans and a tank top, Savy looked like she'd just walked out onto a stage to give a concert to a packed house.

"Can they even do this?" Savy handed a stapled packet of paper to Father Matthews.

Father Matthews's gnarled fingers trembled as he took the documents. Gunny noticed there was some strain at the corners of his eyes. He looked tired like he hadn't been sleeping well.

She wanted to go to him, to fuss over the man that had always been as much a father to her as her own had. In some cases, more of a father than the

General. Because Father Matthews was always just on the other side of the fence.

"They can't kick us out?" asked Savy. "Can they?"

Father Matthews drew in a deep breath as his dark gaze scanned the documents. He had a big heart where Bright Horizons was concerned. That's where all six of his sons had come to him from.

"No, they can't kick you out," said Gunny. "Not if we put up a fight."

They both turned to the door. Gunny came into the screen door without knocking. She'd fairly lived here when she was younger. She couldn't remember a time when she had knocked, less even when the door was locked.

"Gunny? Is that you?" Savy opened her arms, and Gunny embraced her old friend. "What are they feeding you out in the desert? You need to come by for a good meal."

Even though Savy was just a few years older than Gunny, the woman had always had a maternal instinct. Which was likely why, after her career as a singer, she'd returned to the foster home that had taken her and her sisters in when their mother had died.

"Let's worry less about my eating habits and more about how to stop these land-grabbing officials from stealing the foster home. First thing we'll do is start a petition."

Savy threw back her head and laughed. Her dark curls bounced as she did. "If you're on it, then I'm not going to worry about it any longer. I still remember when you chained yourself to the science lab cabinet to protest dissecting frogs."

"It was inhumane."

"It saved my GPA because I knew I'd pass out if I held a scalpel. You home for good?"

"Nope." Gunny shook her head. "I'm here to get married real quick, then I've gotta hop on a plane to Australia. The human population is encroaching on the Brumby population there."

"Right." Savy nodded, but there was clear confusion in her hazel eyes. "Did you say married? Who's the lucky guy?"

"Well..." Gunny turned her attention to Father Matthews, who sat with the documents in his lap. "I was hoping I could convince one of the Matthews boys to be my sacrificial lamb."

Both Savy and Father Matthews blinked.

"Not Charlie, of course," said Gunny.

Savy took a step toward the front door, crossing her arms over her chest. "Oh, that's over. So over."

She cleared her throat once, twice. She opened

her mouth, then closed it. Finally, she affixed a bright smile. But there was a wobble at one side that made the smile look lopsided. Savy James and Charlie Matthews might not be together, but those two were so not over.

"I'll just let the two of you look over that paperwork," Savy said, backpedaling out the door. "I've gotta get back. Who knows what the kids have been up to while I've been gone. Let me know what you find. And good luck with your marriage, Gunny. Thanks, Father Matthews."

She was already in her van before she'd finished speaking. Gunny grinned after the woman as she pulled off. It must've taken Savy a lot of courage to drive out to Flying Cross after her and Charlie's last break-up. But Gunny supposed the woman must've known that the eldest of the Matthews boys wasn't at home.

Gunny turned to Father Matthews. "So, you got any sons hanging around that I can borrow for a few months?"

Father Matthews chuckled, which turned into a cough. Then turned into hacking. Gunny grabbed a tissue box from the fireplace and handed it to him.

"It's nothing, just a little cold." Father Matthews waved the box away and cleared his throat. "None of my boys are here right now. Otherwise, I'd offer one of them up along with some lemonade."

"Well, which one is the closest by? I just need a day, a couple of hours at most."

Father Matthews smiled, but he didn't attempt to laugh. "I'm afraid none of my boys will be back until Thanksgiving at the earliest, which is after your father's deadline."

Gunny cursed—in her head, not under her breath. Father Matthews was not only a father figure to her, he had a direct line to the man upstairs —her father. The last thing Gunny needed was the General haunting her over foul language.

"What's wrong with Truman?" asked Father Matthews. "He's a good man. Certainly good enough to pass your father's muster."

Again, Gunny decided the best tactic was to hold her tongue. The General looked down on lying as much as he looked down on cursing.

"I'm starting to think Abe had a plan all along with those men and his girls. You might grow to love Truman as each of your sisters has grown to love her own young man."

"Love him? I don't even like him. I could very possibly hate him."

"Love and hate are two strong emotions. There's

a very thin line separating the two, which makes it easy to fall from one side to the other."

"Isn't hate the opposite of love?"

"No. That's apathy; which means not caring at all. Besides, you're both leaving soon, heading back to your careers."

Was that why Truman was out shooting this morning? Trying to get back in shipshape so he could take down live targets? Gunny's lip curled at the thought. She could not marry that man. But she just might have to. He was the only man around that could meet her goals and her time frame.

She could marry him and then never see him again. It wouldn't be the worst thing in the world.

CHAPTER SEVEN

It was the worst thing in the world.

Truman never thought he'd see this day. He was getting married. He had to. He had no options left. Not if he wanted to still be of use.

The military wouldn't have him, no matter how many tests the doctors ran. The tear in his shoulder would always show up on x-rays and shout in black and white pixels that he was no longer good enough. There was nowhere to hide from the x-ray. No cover he could take.

So, this was his only option. He'd stay where he was needed. Where he could at least be of use. Here on this ranch.

Maybe it wasn't the worst thing in the world?

Working the ranch was good, honest work. Even

though he was about to come by it on a dishonest route.

Marriage.

To a woman he didn't love.

To a woman he didn't even like. But that was part of combat. Soldiers signed up to do the things that others found distasteful or were too scared to do themselves. All in protection of the many.

At least he would be the only sacrifice for his friends. He owed them that much after failing to spot the bomb that had ruined all their lives and took the general from them. This would be his payment.

He'd lay down his gun and put a ring on Gunnery Silver's finger. Then she'd leave, and the two would likely rarely see each other. She'd head back overseas on whatever animal rights or environmental crusade she was on. He'd stay on the ranch and keep this home front safe. One day they might reunite to sign divorce papers.

That thought left a burn in his chest. Though he wasn't in love with Gunny, he didn't like the idea of divorce. It felt too much like giving up.

"You sure about this?" Linc said as Truman stepped out of the cabin.

The men lined up outside, all dressed in military

finery. It was the last wedding ceremony. There wouldn't be a need to get this gussied up again.

"Yeah," he said. "I'm sure."

Truman had loved serving with these men. It had been the privilege of his life to have their backs in combat. It would be worth it to stand by them now.

"He meant about Gunny," said Jeff. "The two of you don't seem to get along."

Truman shrugged. "We don't have to. We won't be in the same place after this week."

"She's leaving that quick?" asked Jeff.

Her flight was booked. As soon as the ink was dry on the deed to the ranch, she was out. To some place in the Australian Outback. Truman scratched at his chest.

"It's not right. We all fell in love. But you...?"

Truman knew he wasn't meant to fall in love. It wasn't in his character. Not for a man that was so good at hiding and taking out the target. Love's arrow could never find him, and he was fine with that.

Because he was so good at lying in wait, he was also good at sensing danger. He saw Catherine walk up to them, a sly smile on her beautiful face.

"Looks like you're going to make my late

husband's requirements in time," she said. "Just by the skin of your teeth. How convenient."

Her smile was false. It was brittle, like the porcelain of her face. She eyed each of the men in turn, but her gaze latched onto Truman.

There was nowhere for him to hide the sweat on his brow. There was no cover he could take. He was out in the open.

"The other five of you might claim a love match," Catherine continued. "But the PETA princess and a decorated sniper? You can't expect me to believe you two fell in love?"

Truman felt Linc and Jefferson at his back. He could tell when Linc opened his mouth and prepared to stand up for their entire family unit. But this wasn't Linc's place. It was Truman's.

"It's true," he said. "The first time I saw Gunny, I wanted to run in the other direction."

In fact, he had gone in the other direction when she'd walked into the house. It was just as her twin Tilly and Carter were saying their vows. When Truman saw Tilly's twin standing in the doorway, he got the sense that his time as a single man was almost up.

"But over this past week, we spent some time

together." True, that time had been short-lived. But the most impactful of that time they'd spent together had been when Truman had been out shooting. When he'd seen Gunny with his rifle, when he'd held Gunny in his arms, and she'd clicked into place against him. "I knew she was the one for me the moment I touched her. I think that the general knew exactly what he was doing when he paired the six of us with his six daughters."

"My husband was not a romantic," said Catherine. "The man was married five times."

Truman looked at the woman. He really looked at her, which was difficult. There was so much makeup on her face. He wondered if Catherine had ever shown the general the real woman beneath that facade.

Catherine's gaze narrowed as though she knew what was going through Truman's mind. Her frosty glare didn't shake him. He knew when someone was hiding.

"There was something about you that drew him to you," Truman said. "But maybe you hid it away? Maybe he went searching for it? Maybe you never showed him again?"

Catherine jerked back as though Truman had struck her. He supposed his words had struck a chord. But just as quickly as she jerked back did her features settle.

"You and Gunnery are exact opposites," Catherine said. "A sniper and an animal rights activist? The others might have feelings for each other, but the two of you? This is a lie and fake, and it will be found out. If not today, then soon after, and this ranch will be mine."

She turned on her heel and walked away. Not to the field where the cars were parked. She walked toward the backyard, where the ceremony would be held.

There were only a few guests seated. Mostly neighbors from nearby ranches and a few townsfolk to make it look official. Now, Truman and Gunny would have to look at each other like they were officially in love. Or like they at least liked the other's company.

For the past couple of days after agreeing to go through with the fake marriage, he had barely seen his betrothed. Truman spent his days working on Linc's improvement projects in the north pasture. While Gunny had spent her days working with the horses in the eastern pasture. They'd barely seen each other except at dinner time, where they studiously ignored one another.

"You make an excellent point," said Linc. "You and Gunny are hiding from each other. Have either of you shown the other the real you?"

Before Truman could answer, he looked up, and there she was. Gunny stood on the porch in a white sundress and sandals. Her blonde hair was pulled up in a swirly bun with tendrils escaping to frame her face. But the best accessory she wore was a smile.

It was so bright that Truman felt blinded. When she threw her head back and laughed, he forgot how to breathe.

"Never mind." Linc clapped him. "I think you just got your first glimpse."

CHAPTER EIGHT

Gunny never thought this day would come. Not that it couldn't come. She had just never spent any length of time thinking about her wedding day. Yet here she was, standing in a white dress with a bunch of wildflowers in her hands.

She was getting married. It had to be done. But did she really have to wear the dress and heels? Gunny reached down to unstrap one shoe, only to have her twin slap her hand away.

"The shoes stay on," said Tilly.

"You were in cowboy boots for your wedding," Gunny said. "Can't I at least wear boots for mine?"

"Boots won't go with that dress," said Mareen, as she stuck another pin in Gunny's hair.

"Great," said Gunny. "Then let's lose the dress, too."

"You look perfect," said Saylor, slapping Gunny's hand away from the zipper on the side of the dress.

Gunny was surrounded by enemy combatants. She was too far from the exit, and she was out of options.

Despite tracking down and calling each one of the Matthews boys, each had politely turned her down. Well, Joe had laughed until he dropped the phone. Topher had hung up on her, stopped answering when she tried to call back.

So much for all the childhood pacts where they'd sliced open their palms with a pocket knife and spit-shaked on promises. Seemed their oaths to have each other's backs only went so far. And that was not down the aisle.

Gunny would be walking down the aisle toward a stranger. Because even after being home for nearly a week, she and Truman Bates were still nothing more than strangers. And she had no problem keeping it that way.

She would marry him. Her sisters would get the deed to the ranch. Then she would be on the next flight out. And that would be that. She'd likely only see her husband on holidays when she came home. If he was even still around.

"Truman's a good guy," Tilly said to her.

"He's a sniper," said Gunny.

"He was a sniper. He's not anymore. They won't have him back because of his shoulder."

Truman hadn't said as much when they'd agreed to this, but Gunny had suspected. She still remembered him wincing in pain when she'd come upon him at their first meeting. That had been five days ago. Their father's three-month deadline expired at the end of the day today.

They were now pushing it close. But in under an hour, the last Silver daughter would be married. The deed would pass into their hands. And all would be right with this part of the world. That would mean Gunny could leave for another part of the world that needed her.

"All being a sniper proves is that he will always have your back," said Scout, "even when you can't see him."

Gunny didn't need Truman to have her back. Because by next week, all he would be seeing would be the back of her.

"You should be in love," said Tilly with a wistful

sigh of a woman who saw cartoon hearts anytime she looked into the blue sky.

All of her sisters were starry-eyed with bubbling, floaty hearts. But all of her sisters wanted to be tied down to one place and push out babies. That had never been Gunny's dream. Gunny's roots were planted deep on this ranch, but she had always wanted to fly free and far.

The truth was, Gunny didn't want love. Love was a powerful feeling. She'd felt it with her birth mother, even though she couldn't remember her. Then she'd passed.

She'd felt it with her second mother, Sarah, as if the woman were her own flesh and blood. And then she'd passed. Each time Gunny's heart had broken. With her father's death, she was certain another crack would leave the organ irreparable.

What man would look twice at a woman with a broken heart? Or even once at a woman who vowed never to have children of her own? Or even blink at a woman who could never love him?

Gunny only had space in her heart for her sisters, her work, and this ranch. She was full up. Luckily, she was gussied up enough to be a presentable bride.

"Can we get this show on the road?" she said.

Gunny stood, and her sisters backed off. Behind her, she heard much sighing and oohing and ahhing. Gunny ignored her sentimental sisters and stomped toward the back door. Only to remember that she was wearing heels and, when she stomped her heels the shoes pinched her toes.

The backyard was filled with a few people from town. She recognized a few faces from this distance, but most were a blur. Before she could get any closer, a tall, dark figure slipped in front of her.

She looked up to see Truman. He was smiling down at her. Those gray eyes bright. Those full lips curved up as though they held a secret, a secret she wanted to know. The flash of teeth he showed her was so dazzling that it momentarily stunned her. That had to be why she didn't protest when he scooped her into his arms and twirled her.

He twirled her. Like, around in a circle. With her feet off the ground and her full weight in his arms. She had never been twirled. She wasn't that kind of girl.

She heard a grunt of pain from him. It must be from the shoulder injury he still hadn't told her about. She weighed more than his rifle. So what was he thinking?

Truman set her feet on the ground. But she was

wearing heels, and the weight distribution was all wrong.

Thankfully, he didn't let her go. He pulled her to him and whispered something in her ear. Before her brain could make out his words, his mouth moved from the cone of her ear, brushed the contours of her cheek, and then his lips were covering hers.

Truman was kissing her. It started as just a light peck on the lips. On another day, that wouldn't have been a big deal. Gunny had been kissed before. She'd never enjoyed the encounters and put a stop to them years ago. She hadn't seen the point of dating when she found most men useless.

But Truman's lips? They were plush, like a down pillow. It was nice to rest against them. She felt as though she could lay right where they stood and take a nap against his mouth.

Except there was also the heat. There was a warmth to Truman's mouth. As though he'd just had a warm cup of morning coffee and was now spreading that curling steam that came with a good cuppa through her.

Man, that was pleasant. The curling hot tendrils of coffee layered over the plush of a pillow. Did other guys know that kissing could be like this? Truman must have kept the secret of kissing all to himself. Otherwise, women would be throwing their faces at him as he walked down the street.

Then he was pulling away. Taking that delicious heat and snuggable pillow with him.

Gunny wrapped her arms around his neck. She just needed one more touch of warmth, one more second of lush comfort.

Truman didn't resist. He leaned into her. Introducing his hands and arms to the game. The embrace took the kiss to the next level. Until the sounds of whoops and catcalls pulled them apart.

"You two can't wait a few minutes until you at least get to the altar?"

Gunny wasn't sure who said it. Her brain was still trying to rewire itself from that kiss. That kiss. What had that kiss been about?

CHAPTER NINE

He hadn't meant to do that. Well, he had. But he hadn't meant to let it get that far.

That kiss. Man, that kiss.

Was it over? Truman wasn't sure? He could still feel the impact of Gunny on his lips. Hot and spicy with an earthy kick to it that he shouldn't have liked, but he desperately wanted another taste of.

Truman, trained soldier that he was, had not been prepared for that. He'd been in areas that were bombed, and he hadn't felt as shaken as he had at the impact of her lips. Bullets had whizzed past his head, but his heart hadn't raced this much.

When he let her go, he was shell-shocked. His

body felt fractured, as though he were coming apart at the seams.

He had just meant to give her a light peck for show. Now hunger claimed him.

It had to be because he hadn't been with a woman in so long. He'd been so focused on healing his injury and getting back into the game. He hadn't had time to date. But that one long moment of having Gunnery Silver in his arms had shattered him.

And so help him, he wanted more.

Gunny was looking at him with a startled expression. Under that startled expression, he saw the unmistakable spark of desire. And she was rattled by it. By the looks of her, she was far more rattled than he was.

She wanted him too. Was that even possible for two people who were so different from one another? For two people who didn't even like one another? For two people who had planned a union where they would be on opposite sides of the world from one another?

Truman took a step back. But his legs weren't working. His hands were still holding onto her. Because he was never letting her go.

Just let her try to get on that plane next week.

Either he would find a way to keep her here with him. Or he would be riding shotgun beside her.

First, he had to get them both down the aisle so he would have the right to be wherever she was.

"Are we doing this?" Truman asked.

"It's the only option," Gunny said after clearing her throat.

Right. The only option. He saw Catherine seated at the back of the rows of seats. She looked smug as though the show of affection hadn't convinced her.

Well, it had convinced him. Truman was hoping maybe it had convinced Gunny. After he'd whispered in her ear that Catherine was here and watching, he had expected Gunny to play-act with just a peck. But she'd thrown herself into that kiss with everything she had. So maybe she would give a piece of herself to him?

Their steps were steady as they walked down the aisle toward Father Matthews. Truman hated being visible to so many eyes. He was used to being in the shadows or behind bushes. He wasn't used to being so visible. In the back of his mind, he kept searching out places where he could hide and blend in. But he couldn't do that. Not when he was the star of the show.

He decided to focus on his friends at the front.

That's why he was doing this, why he was placing himself in such a vulnerable position. This wedding, this marriage, was to protect his friends. It was supposed to be a sham. Only, with every step he took, it felt more and more real.

Truman's grip tightened on Gunny's arm. He liked the feel of her fingers tucked inside his elbow. Her index finger pressed against his bicep like it was a trigger aiming him forward. They came to a stop when they reached Father Matthews.

The old man smiled down at them. Truman noted the dark circles under the man's eyes. There was also a fine sheen of sweat on his forehead in the overcast sky.

Father Matthews loved these girls like they were his own. The stress of these last few months must've taken its toll on him as well as the Silvers. After this, they would all be able to rest easy.

"Dearly beloved," said Father Matthews. "I was there as each of these girls came into the world. Their parents passed them onto me and asked me to look after them as I would my own as their godfather. I have done that. I've handed each off to the man who became her husband. This is my last official job as their caretaker. I will be going on a much-needed vacation after this ceremony."

A light rumble of laughter went through the crowd. Gunny smiled up at the man who was her godfather. Truman was entirely captivated by her smile. His mind reeled with tactics on how to trigger such a reaction with her that was aimed solely at him.

"The couple has provided their own vows," Father Matthews was saying.

They had? This was news to Truman, since he hadn't written anything down to provide. He slid a glance over at Gunny, who smirked as she avoided his gaze. Truman knew then and there that life with this woman was going to be interesting.

"As is the Tibetan Buddhist way—"

Wait! Buddhist? Who was Buddhist?

Gunny's grin spread in a way that didn't read peaceful to him. It was all mischief.

"—the couple will answer the first set of vows together."

Oh? That didn't sound so bad. Truman had expected chanting and candles and chakra alignments. Call and response he could deal with.

"Truman and Gunnery, do you pledge to help each other to develop your hearts and minds, cultivating generosity, ethics, patience, enthusiasm, concentration, and wisdom as you age and undergo the various ups and downs of life, and to transform them into the path of love, compassion, joy, and equanimity?"

"We do," said Gunny.

Truman was still stuck on *developing his heart and mind*. What did any of that mumbo jumbo even mean? But in the silence, which was peppered with snickers from the men in his unit and the thudding taps from their wives to be quiet, Truman realized he had to answer.

"I… I mean, we do."

Father Matthews nodded sagely. He wiped at his forehead, catching sweat there with a cloth, and then continuing on. "Recognizing that the external conditions in life will not always be smooth and that internally your own minds and emotions will some-times get stuck in negativity, do you pledge to see all these circumstances as a challenge to help you grow, to open your hearts, to accept yourselves, and each other; and to generate compassion for others who are suffering?"

Generate compassion for others? Was he getting married or opening an animal shelter?

"We do," said Gunny. Her own lips twitching along with her brothers'-in-law.

Was she for real? Or was Truman getting

punked? It didn't matter because his gaze was fixed on her mouth.

What Truman realized was there would be a part of this ceremony where he would get to kiss that mouth again. Having his lips pressed against hers was worth any vow he was making, even if it was to some elephant-headed god and many-armed goddess.

"We do," Truman agreed.

Truman had to wait a long minute for the next section as Father Matthews took a minute to clear his throat. And then grabbed a water bottle for a lengthy sip. The man was reading a tome with words that didn't go together, so Truman didn't begrudge the man his need for a brief interlude between passages.

"Understanding that just as we are a mystery to ourselves, each other person is also a mystery to us, do you pledge to seek to understand yourselves, each other, and all living beings, to examine your own minds continually and to regard all the mysteries of life with curiosity and joy?"

Now Gunny was out and out smiling at the confused look on Truman's face. Truman let the words roll over him. He would simply have Gunny explain their meanings later. While she did, he'd have the pleasure of watching her lips press together and open. He'd lie in wait, hiding in plain sight, until he could make his attack and kiss her soundly to satisfy his curiosity and joy.

"We do," he said.

"Do you pledge to preserve and enrich your affection for each other and to share it with all beings? To take the loving feelings you have for one another and your vision of each other's potential and inner beauty as an example, rather than spiraling inwards and becoming self-absorbed, to radiate this love outwards to all beings?"

"We..." It was Gunny who hesitated now.

Truman found he actually liked that part. Something in his heart told him that loving feelings for this woman was within reach. He wanted to spiral toward her. He was already becoming self-absorbed in everything she did. He was certain his growing feelings for her were radiating outward.

"We do," both Gunny and Truman said.

They stared at each other in silence. The silence seemed to stretch. Was that it? Were they done pledging their intentions and afterlives and next lives so that they could get to the good part? Surely, there had to be a part where they were pronounced man and wife, and he could kiss the bride.

Truman looked over to Father Matthews to determine the hold-up. The man seemed to be struggling for breath. One of Father Matthews' hands was clutching his Bible, the other his heart. In slow motion, the older man's body began to crumple.

Truman let go of Gunny and reached for him before the man hit the ground. "Call an ambulance," he shouted at his friends. "He's having a heart attack."

CHAPTER TEN

he smell of antiseptic made the hairs of Gunny's nostrils burn. The yellow of the fluorescent lights hurt her eyes. The intermittent beeping and squeak of shoes on linoleum made her head throb.

She'd been in too many hospitals in her life. She began her life in a hospital as a preemie as her mother lay dying down the hall. She'd been back to the hospital when Tessa Matthews sickened with breast cancer. The last time she'd been here was with Sarah, the woman who had raised Gunny and Tilly as if they were her own flesh and blood.

Gunny had mourned Sarah's loss as though her heart had been ripped from her chest. Her father had prepared them all for the possibility of him making the ultimate sacrifice. It had never occurred to Gunny that Sarah could be taken from her. And then, in a blink, she was gone.

If memory served her correctly, Gunny had been sitting in this very hall when the doctors had come to tell the Silvers of Sarah's passing. Gunny thought she remembered staring at the same painting on the wall when she'd come to visit Tessa Matthews for the last time. And now she was waiting for word of her second father, the last parental figure she had in this world.

The ticking of the clock was in tune with the pounding of her temples. Already it was late at night. Or maybe it was the next day? She wasn't sure? The hands of the clock blurred, and Gunny didn't have the energy to make out which was the hour and minute hand. Not that it mattered.

They'd been here for hours and still no word on Father Matthews. The doctors had wheeled him into an OR upon arrival. The doors had closed, and they were all left on the other side, waiting.

A shiver skittered across Gunny's shoulders. The large waiting room was cold, with AC units blasting. Alternately a burst of hot would knock her back to the wall when the sliding glass doors that led to the outside world opened to admit new patients and visitors. The mix of cold and hot left the air tepid for a time. Until, for a long time, the doors to the outside world stayed shut, and the cold got under her skin.

Arms came around Gunny's shoulders from behind. She wasn't sure which of her sisters embraced her. She didn't care. Their body blocked the AC vents, shielding Gunny from the blast of cold air. Gunny needed the reprieve from the chill to get her bearings.

She hated this part. The part where she had to hold still and wait for the results. That's why she was always mobile. She started the fight, and then once everything was in motion, she moved on and left the battle to others.

She'd gotten Father Matthews to the hospital. She'd raised her voice until she got the attention of everyone in scrubs or a white coat to get Father Matthews the attention he needed. Now the fight was in the OR, in the hands of the very best surgeon in town.

Gunny's work here was done. It was time to move on. Time to find a new fight.

Except she couldn't move. She didn't want to move. Not yet. Her sister's arms bade every cell in her body to wait, to rest, to relax. Those arms whispered that she wasn't alone, never had been, never would be.

It was probably Tilly holding her up. The two had come into this world together. A pang of guilt pinched Gunny in the chest that she didn't always stay in constant contact with her twin. It wasn't for lack of a satellite link -not in today's interconnected world. Often, Gunny simply found it easier to be on her own.

Looking across the waiting room, she saw Tilly wrapped in Carter's arms. In fact, all of her sisters were wrapped up in their husband's arms. So who was holding Gunny?

Truman.

She had completely forgotten about Truman. The man who had just pledged himself to examine the mysteries of life as well as both their inner beauties together. Gunny almost snorted at the memory of his face when he'd heard those vows. She'd pulled them off the internet the day before. She'd figured if they were going to pledge themselves in this ridiculous union, then their vows should be ridiculous.

Although his strong arms, the comfort of his chest, the strong beat of his heart against her spine, none of that felt ridiculous right now. It felt right. It felt necessary.

Gunny took a step away from him. She didn't get far. The effort was halfhearted to begin with, so it ended with her pivoting in his embrace to face him.

He looked tired. There were creases at the edges of his eyes. His lashes covered half of his gray eyes like a window shade had been pulled down at sunset.

Her gaze lowered to his mouth. His top lip rested on his bottom lip, like a soft pillow atop a firm mattress. Gunny knew the two textures of his mouth. She vividly remembered the softness, the insistence, the hunger.

Her face heated. She lifted her heel to step away from him. Before her toes could leave the floor, Truman tightened his embrace.

"He's strong," said Truman. "He'll come out of this."

Gunny shook her head. "My mother was strong, both of them. And they both died here."

Truman didn't argue with her. He pulled her closer. A hand lifted to her temple. He brushed a few tendrils that had come undone from her updo out of her eyes. The light brush of his fingertips stopped the pounding in her temple.

It was too familiar. It was too comfortable. Gunny didn't do attachments. It was hard to fight while being weighed down by another body. And she needed to fight. She needed a cause. Some corporate demon to shout at. A tree to chain herself to. A pen to write a strongly worded letter.

"My dad was strong too," she said. "But he was taken out by a bomb."

Truman stiffened. When he did, his hold on her loosened. Finally, she was able to pull away.

It was clear by the stony look on his face that she'd struck a nerve. Well, it was better this way. No attachments. She might be one who saved lives, but she was far from a nurturer. Best her husband learn that now.

CHAPTER ELEVEN

*H*e was stalking her. He wasn't ashamed to admit it. She was hard not to follow. White dress and heels. There was no camouflaging someone like her.

Truman's gaze tracked Gunny as she walked down the street and away from the hospital. Her sisters had started to protest her leaving, but when they'd seen Truman on her heels, they'd all quieted.

It was good that they all trusted her safety to him. Not that there was much danger out in the small midwestern town. Even if Gunny had decided to walk through the nursery, Truman would've followed.

He wondered if those vows of hers had cast some sort of spell on him. By agreeing to understand the mystery of her, to examine her mind, had he irrevocably linked his soul to hers.

Well, they were married. So he supposed so. Despite their particular brand of vows not including the phrase, he was still honor-bound to protect her. Because more than anything, Truman wanted to have Gunny. He wanted to hold her. To comfort her, of course.

Father Matthews would recover. The man was a warrior. His heart was too big to give out. It would mend.

Then Gunny would have no reason to stay. She would leave. Which was the plan.

So why was Truman clenching his fists?

As Gunny ambled down the street, Truman saw men leering at her as she walked by. True, she was wearing a white wedding dress. Those slender shoulders were exposed for the world to see. The toned muscles of her arms made Truman's mouth water.

Yes, he wanted to hold his wife. More than that, he wanted to feel her strong arms around him. And he definitely wanted to taste that lush mouth again.

One of the leering men craned his neck all the way to get another look at her. When the leerer's shoulders followed his head, Truman picked up his step. He caught the man's bicep in a grip before the pervert could take a step toward Truman's wife. The look in Truman's gaze screamed *Mine*. The man must have heard it loud and clear because he put his hands up in surrender and backed off.

Truman picked up the pursuit of his prey. But Gunny had disappeared. There weren't many places she could've escaped to.

There was a florist shop setting out bouquets on an outdoor display. The ice cream shop wasn't yet opened. Surprisingly, the bar was.

The bell over the door still jingled, leading Truman to believe that that was Gunny's likely destination. He slipped inside the establishment but didn't spot a woman in a white wedding dress.

He'd lost her. How had she gotten past him? Truman had never missed a shot. Even now, his hand itched for a weapon that wasn't at his side. His shoulder ached, but not from any of the strain of the previous day's events. Truman ached to have Gunny back in his arms.

He caught a flash of white across the street. Looking up, he saw the town hall. It was the only other place that she could've ducked into. Truman dashed up the steps, keeping to the shadows at the side of the building out of habit.

He slipped inside behind a man in a suit with a briefcase. Not that Truman could blend in much. He was dressed in uniform. But no one gave him a second look. Truman doubted he would've noticed in any regards. He scanned the room, his gaze like a scope. When he saw her moving with purpose toward a man behind a desk, Truman stalked toward her.

He no longer bothered to stay out of sight. He wanted everyone around to know that he was on the hunt. His prey was within his crosshairs.

"Excuse me?" Gunny said.

The man with a young face but a thinning hairline turned. He wore a bright customer service smile. That smile dropped the moment his gaze locked on Gunny.

"Oh, no." His shoulders slumped. "You're back."

"What?" said Gunny.

"Tilly?"

"No. I'm Gunny."

"Gunnery? Gunny Silver? Is that you?" The smile crept back over his face, unwrinkling his features. "It's me, Ryan Burns. From high school. I dated your sister."

"Okay," Gunny said noncommittally.

"We were pretty serious for a couple weekends."

"Sure. Fine. Listen, Ron."

"Ryan," he corrected, leaning in. "So, how've you been?"

Truman didn't like the way the man's gaze roamed over his wife's form. It looked like he was about to put the moves on her. Then the man's gaze widened as he took in her state of dress.

"You're in a wedding dress?"

Gunny took a step back from the desk. She ran her hands down her dress as though just remembering that she was wearing the garment. Then she put her hands on her hips. Before she could speak, the clerk went on.

"Don't tell me you're here to get married. Your sister was in here last week."

"I'm already married." Gunny waved her hands as though it was an inconvenient truth.

"You're married? Who's the guy? Another soldier?" The clerk looked up. Likely because he felt Truman's glare. "To him?"

Gunny looked over her shoulder. The pose she struck when she looked at him reminded Truman of a blonde-haired Wonder Woman. All she needed was the lasso of truth on her hip. Not that he needed to be roped in. He was already wound tight around her finger, as evidenced by his need to be near her.

She frowned at Truman. She only spared him the one glance before turning her attention back to Ryan, the clerk.

"Ron." She snapped her fingers to get his attention. "I'm here to file a petition. The government is trying to take over the Clearwater Valley lands where the Bright Horizon's Foster Home is."

Ryan blinked and then smiled. "You know, I remember back in middle school when you protested that Harry Potter got banned from the library by the PTA."

He leaned to the side to speak directly to Truman. The clerk chucked a thumb at Gunny as he spoke, as though he and Truman were sharing an inside joke and leaving her out.

"The moms were opposed to the evils of magic in the book, but Gunny wrote up a speech about censorship that made it into the local paper. Then after reading the book, she launched another protest because the books dealt with the enslavement of elves."

Yup, that sounded like the woman Truman was coming to know. But to make sure this guy didn't think he sided with him, Truman stepped up beside Gunny. He placed a hand at her low back. In his mind, he heard a click, like the safety being set to the off position. All pistons were ready to fire. He just needed to remove the obstruction out of the way.

"Ron, will you go and get my wife the paperwork she needs?"

Ryan opened his mouth, likely to correct Truman on his name. It was likely the expression on Truman's face that let him know that neither Truman nor Gunny could care any less. The man turned on his heel and disappeared into another room.

"You following me?" Gunny asked.

"Yes," Truman admitted.

"Just because we're married doesn't give you the rights to my business."

Actually, it did. But Truman didn't want to argue that. "We've all had a shock with Father Matthews's heart attack. I didn't want you to be alone."

"I don't need you to coddle me, Truman. I can take care of myself."

She crossed her arms over her chest, but she didn't back away from his touch. Instead, she seemed to sink deeper into the palm of his hand. Before she had a chance to respond, Ryan came back out.

"You can't file a petition on the Clearwater Valley lands," said Ryan.

"Why not?" said Gunny. "It's my First Amendment right."

"Well, yeah. It is. It's just that you already filed a petition years ago. Looks like it's been approved."

"What?" Gunny snatched the documents from him.

"Yup, says there the federal government has approved the Clearwater lands as protected property since they have wild horses running on them. Congratulations."

CHAPTER TWELVE

Gunny felt the walls closing in on her. She couldn't draw in a deep breath to fill her lungs. Her legs felt like jelly as she tried to move. To get away from the walls. To find a place where she could breathe.

The dress she was wearing felt itchy on her skin. The shoes she wore pinched her toes. The pins in her hair made her temples throb.

She needed to get out. To get away. To shout. To raise her fist.

But at who? And to what end?

Finally, she found the door to the building and pushed through. The sun warmed her face, but the rays didn't penetrate through to her shivering bones.

The fresh air hit her nostrils, but she couldn't gulp down enough.

If she couldn't breathe, she couldn't shout. If she couldn't shout, she couldn't launch into a formal protest. Protesting is what had gotten her here.

It was all her fault. She'd saved the wild horses, which was great. Those majestic creatures needed a hero. But so did the kids at the foster home.

Gunny turned in a circle. She was unsure which way to go. In the end, strong arms stopped any forward motion and pulled her into a cocoon of firm, cushiony muscles.

The hard and soft sensations further scrambled Gunny's brain. That had to be why she didn't fight being overtaken. She surrendered to Truman as he brought her tightly against him.

"Breathe," he crooned. "Just breathe. I've got you."

She didn't need him to have her. She was woman. Hear her roar. Instead, what came out of her was a whimper.

"This is my fault." The words were said into Truman's chest. "Those kids are going to lose the only home they know. And it's all my fault."

"You were trying to do a good thing for the horses. Sometimes there's only the choice between the best bad option or the irreconcilable good."

His words weren't making much sense. The only bad or good option she wanted right now was to not move from this space. It was bad to let him hold her like this. After all, Gunny was getting on a plane in just a few days. But right now, in this moment, it simply felt so good to let someone else have her back.

"Seems to me," Truman went on, "either the horses have to move or the people do."

Two bad decisions. The horses had roamed that land for decades. Over the years, their habitat had been threatened by the encroachment of humanity. The resources they thrived on were in stark competition with herded cattle and domesticated horses. Their long-term survival was in serious jeopardy.

The same could be said for the kids that Savy and her sisters took care of at Bright Horizons. The place was a haven for kids who were sent from the inner cities, often as a last resort. The James girls worked magic that reform schools and juvenile halls envied. It was no wonder. They'd come up out of the foster care system in that same house years ago.

"If the paperwork is already filed, there is no choice," Gunny said.

She knew what she had to do. But before she did it, she allowed herself one last second in Truman's embrace. One last deep inhale of his heady scent of outdoor and aftershave. One last circular rub by his hand at her low back.

Then she took a step back. Truman let her go, but not far. He continued to crowd her space like he belonged beside her.

"Where are you going?" he said as she turned to walk down the street.

"To talk to Savy and her sisters."

"I'll drive you."

"I can walk."

"In those shoes?"

They both looked down at her heels. The white shoes were smudged from her walk to city hall. They wouldn't survive the trek across town to the foster home.

"Fine," she said.

They walked in silence back to the hospital. At some point, his hand returned to her low back. Gunny decided she'd allow it. Only because of the high heels and cracks in the sidewalks.

She was going to have to break Truman of this habit soon. She'd be leaving him in a few days. His sure fingers would be far beyond her low back by then. And wasn't that too bad.

Gunny had never wanted a husband. Had never

actually given the matter any thought until the reading of her father's will. Now that she had one, it didn't seem all that bad.

She'd especially liked that bit with the kissing. Truman had had both his hands on her body at that time. One at her upper back and one at her lower back.

She should've offered up a protest then, but she hadn't been able to find the words. No, she hadn't wanted to find the words. Because she'd liked his mouth against hers.

Maybe she could get another kiss out of him before she had to leave? It wouldn't be too much to ask for a goodbye kiss. Would it?

They arrived at the hospital parking lot. Truman opened the passenger door of his truck for her. Gunny climbed inside and slumped back into the bucket seat. It had already been an eventful morning, and the late afternoon was looking bleak.

Had she really only gotten married just earlier today? Her dress looked like she'd been out working the ranch. She'd told her sisters it was pointless to put her in white. But this day had been more about them than it was about her. She'd saved the day with her vows. She'd saved her home with one set of words, but another family would suffer because of words she'd said long ago.

The truck pulled up to the outskirts of the town. The paved street ended a mile back. The dust cloud of gravel still plumed behind the truck from the dirt road. The Bright Horizon's Foster Home was just on the edge of civilization before the land went to all things wild. The town's residents preferred it that way. The kids who wound up at the foster home were often more feral than anything. Gunny knew that firsthand. She'd grown up next to six prior residents.

Truman put the truck in park. Gunny didn't immediately leap out of her seat. She stared beyond the dilapidated ranch house to the splendor that surrounded it. Brown earth bloomed into green foliage that raced up blue mountains capped with white clouds. It looked like a dream world where peace came for a holiday. But the raised voices, racing feet, and banging could be heard from inside the house, which shook with activity.

The natives were restless. Which made this the best time to go in. Savy and her sisters would be distracted with the rambunctious kids they managed.

Gunny's foot tapped against a metal box. She

looked down and noticed that her heel had become hooked on the handle. She reached down, but Truman beat her to it.

"Let me get that for you," he said, brushing her hands away.

Their hands and her foot tangled together. As fingers and heels lifted and tugged, Gunny's shoe came off, and the metal box clanged open. The contents that spilled out turned Gunny's blood cold.

"It's secure," he said.

"Not if my shoe could free it. Why do you even have a gun in the car?"

"I always have a gun."

"Were you armed at our ceremony this morning?"

"Are we going inside?"

Gunny noticed he didn't answer her question. Instead, he reached down to shove the metal box back under the passenger seat.

"You can't leave that here," she protested. "There are children inside."

Truman gave her an exasperated look. He brought the gun out of the box, pulled out the magazine. Checking the safety, he put the gun in his back waistband and the magazine in his pocket.

"Satisfied?" he asked.

Gunny wanted to tell him that she would be satisfied if there were no longer any guns on the planet. But she had a bigger battle coming. She'd need all her strength to face the James sisters and tell them it was her fault they were losing the only home they'd ever known.

CHAPTER THIRTEEN

The steel of the gun was cold against his low back. He could feel the heat of Gunny's glare on it as he climbed out of the truck. He rounded to the passenger side door to help her out. Of course, she'd already hopped down and was headed for the ranch-style house that looked like a strong wind would blow it over.

When he caught up to her, Gunny turned and looked at him quizzically. "You can go. I'll find my way back."

"I'm not leaving you out here in the middle of nowhere," he said. "Shoes, remember?"

She didn't look down. She glared at him, hands on her hips just like the first time she'd stood over him. "I've spent most of my adult life out in the middle of nowhere."

"Well, now you're my wife, and I'm rolling with you."

"Are you going to keep throwing that in my face?"

"Throwing what in your face?"

"The matrimony thing. You realize it's temporary."

All his life, Truman Bates had been known as a calm person. His mother had told him he rarely cried as a baby. His grandmother, who'd raised him after his mother's untimely death, often bragged to her Canasta friends that her grandson never once threw a tantrum. As a young man, Truman never raised his voice in the heat of an argument because he rarely found reason to debate.

Things had always been black or white for him. Never shades of gray. The haze of gray was a place where disagreements could brew. So, Truman never ventured there.

Until this past week when he agreed to this fake marriage with Gunnery Silver.

It should've been cut and dry. Instead, it was a whole, wet mess of feelings in his chest that alternately warmed and went cold. He constantly wanted to push her away and pull her close. He wanted to hear her voice, but none of the arguments. He wanted to gaze into those clear blue eyes but not deal with any of the judgment. And he couldn't for the life of him remember when he'd promised her temporary?

Gunny could call him temporary all she wanted. What she'd soon learn was that her new husband had the patience of a tiger, an animal that moved slowly and quietly, stalking their prey for extended periods of time before pouncing. Gunny was in Truman's crosshairs, and she would soon learn that he never missed a shot.

For now, he stayed quiet. He watched and waited. Meanwhile, she snuck glances at him as they climbed the porch steps.

Truman was really liking the annoyed pinch she got to her mouth. He wondered if he caught her lip, if he could straighten that pout out? He really wanted to try. But the woman wouldn't even let him open a door for her. He doubted she'd let him steal another kiss.

The house shook with a thundering boom. Truman pulled Gunny into his arms, pressing her face into his chest. A child wailed. Another screamed the word *no.* Then a calm voice of reason interjected between the two.

"Either you two work it out amongst yourselves with words, or I will bring out scissors, and we'll handle this like the good King Solomon."

"But Ms. Savy, it's *miiiiiine,*" screeched the wailer.

"It's not yours," said a slightly less high-pitched voice. "You're an orphan, so you can't own anything."

"That's enough out of both of you," said the reasonable adult by the name of Savy. "Keep it up, and you'll be eating Ms. Tricksy's cooking for dinner."

The wailing and moaning stopped instantly.

"Thought so," said Ms. Savy, in a chipper, singsong tone that reminded Truman of Mary Poppins.

"If you're done feeling me up?"

That voice was not the soprano of Julie Andrews or Ms. Savy. Truman looked down at Gunny. She had a quizzical expression on her face. But he wasn't looking at her whole face. He was looking at her lips. That sassy mouth was so close to his. He could taste her breath. He remembered the sweetness he'd found there this morning, the peace that whispered on her breath. He wanted to press them both into the wall and stay hidden there while he kissed her senseless.

Gunny's breath caught, as though she knew exactly what he wanted to do. She didn't push him away.

"Ms. Savy, there are people making out in the parlor."

That childish voice made Truman let go of his hold on Gunny. But he didn't back off completely. He stayed at her flank. These kids were clearly out of control, and he wasn't sure how many of them there were. Whoever the kid was that called them out dashed around a corner before Truman could get a good look at them. The shouting was coming from the right. He heard footsteps to the left as well.

A dark head of curls came at them from the right. Ms. Savy was a tall drink of water with golden tanned skin that called to an island climate. Her hazel gaze had a tilt that matched the curve of her full lips. Her footsteps faltered and her bright smile dimmed when she saw Gunny.

"Did you come from the hospital?"

"No," said Gunny. "Oh, God no. He's fine. Well, not fine." Gunny took a breath and tried to start again, but Truman picked up the mantle instead.

"It was a heart attack," he said. "He's in stable condition, but he hasn't woken up yet."

Savy nodded at Truman before returning her gaze to Gunny. "The boys?"

"Charlie and Joe should be here by tonight."

Savy nodded again. She twisted a band on her left ring finger. It wasn't gold or silver. It looked like plastic, like it came from a Cracker Jack box or toy store.

"And who is this?" asked Savy, her gaze landing on Truman as she twisted her ring.

"This is Truman," said Gunny. "He's my... husband."

Savy raised a brow. Her lip followed the same upward curve of approval. "Good luck with that."

Truman wasn't sure who Savy directed the comment to. He decided to take it as a well-wish for a long and happy marriage. Because that's now what he intended to get out of this union.

"If you're not here about Father Matthews, then you must have found something out about the government's rights over this land."

Gunny nodded, but she didn't say anything else. Just as she opened her mouth, another crash filled the silence. Followed by a yelp and a string of curses that no child should know.

Both Gunny and Truman looked to the left. Savy ignored the crash and the language. Her attention stayed on Gunny.

"Well?" prompted Savy. "Did you find a way out of this?"

"I found the original petition. It was filed years ago."

"Okay, that's a start. No one knows their way around a petition like you."

Gunny took a deep breath, let it out, then took one more. "The original petition was filed by me."

CHAPTER FOURTEEN

Gunny closed the door behind her. The moment she did, the shouts and yelling of the kids began up again. Before that there had been fifteen minutes of silence.

Not a blessed silence. There had been nothing peaceful about the quiet conversation Gunny had had with Savy. It had been a tense one-sided conversation where Gunny had to *mea culpa* for a cause she believed in, a cause which was her very life's purpose -saving wild horses from humanity's encroaching progress.

Gunny stumbled over her words as she showed Savy the five-year-old petition that Gunny had drafted as a high school senior with dreams of changing the world. Or at least the valley beyond the borders of the Silver Star Ranch and the Flying Cross Ranch. Seventeen-year-old Gunny hadn't known that the Bright Horizons Foster Home, the place where the Matthews boys had spent the start of their lives, and the James sisters had come back to take over, sat just at the edge of Clearwater Valley where the wild horses ran free.

What was the saying? Ignorance of the law excuses no one.

"I'm so sorry, Savy."

"You didn't do this on purpose."

Savy reached out and squeezed Gunny's shoulder, but the move was halfhearted. Like a mother giving a child an absent pat on the head while they looked over the stack of unpaid bills on the table. Savy had bigger concerns to worry over than the paper Gunny had written years ago.

One by one, heads poked around corners and out of cracked doorways.

"Are we gonna be homeless again?"

"Ashton's going back to juvie."

"They'll probably split us apart."

"Noooo, I don't want you to leave, Denny."

"That's enough you all." Savy clapped her hands in quick succession. She didn't raise her voice, but her words carried. In the silence, she turned back to Gunny. "Let me deal with this. We'll catch up later."

Gunny wanted to tell the kids that the fight wasn't over. This was just the first round. Unfortunately, they didn't have years to wait and come back around for another bout. They'd have to be out in months, maybe weeks.

There was a part of Gunny that wanted to stay, to figure out a strategy and fight. But she'd already done enough. Her helpfulness was what got them here. She felt a tug toward the door, and the shame in her allowed herself to be pulled.

The moment the door closed behind her, the children's voices erupted again. It sounded like wild animals had been let out of their cages. She didn't envy Savvy her job. Animals weren't that noisy out in the wild. Their lives depended on their silence.

Truman walked beside her, quiet as a mouse tiptoeing around lions. That was one thing Gunny could say about her husband. He didn't make a lot of noise.

Her husband. This man was her husband. It appeared the bonds of matrimony were tight because she couldn't seem to shake him.

He had been a steady presence beside her all day. Truman had been the one to catch Father Matthews before he'd hit the ground. He'd done CPR to ensure there were life signs while they waited for the paramedics. Meanwhile, Gunny and her sisters had stood by in horror as the man who had been often closer than their father struggled to breathe.

Gunny stumbled now as the memories assaulted her. Coupled with the guilt over the petition and she lost her footing. Truman's arms were around her, bringing her into his hold.

She knew she should fight to get away from him. She didn't want to be this close to anyone right now. She felt so weak, so weary.

"I'm fine," she said. Although she wasn't sure she was loud enough. Even her voice was wobbly, weighed down by the stress and strain of the day.

"I think we should get you home," he said. "You've had a long day."

Truman's arms tightened around her. Instead of feeling trapped in a vise, she felt as though she were being tucked into a bed made of memory foam. Soft and firm at the same time, his chest seemed to conform to her body.

Which would be impossible since they'd never done this before. He'd never held her or wrapped her up tightly like she was precious. He'd never tucked her head against his heart and rested his cheek at her temple. So why did it all feel so familiar, like they'd been doing this for years? Why did it all feel so right?

"I don't want to go home just yet," she said after long moments in his embrace. "I need some fresh air."

It wasn't lost on Gunny that they were standing outside. The freshest air in the valley lifted the escaped tendrils of her hair. Truman loosened his hold on her. Slowly, like a tricky knot unraveling.

Once they were disentangled, he looked down at her. She couldn't meet his gaze. Instead, she turned on her heel and started off down the trail.

She would be the first to admit that traversing through the wild in heels wasn't the smartest thing in the world. But she wasn't going to admit that out loud today. She picked her way carefully on the well-tread path. Truman gave her some space but kept her within arm's reach.

"You don't have to follow me."

"It's beautiful out here," he said.

His gaze was on his surroundings, but Gunny got the sense that he kept one eye on her. In the far-off distance, a lone horse grazed on a patch of green grass at the edge of a watering hole. To the far end of the water, more of the herd rested or drank. The horses were a rainbow of stark whites, mahogany browns, and midnight blacks. The animals had no idea that a long-fought battle had been won for them. Or that their champion had caused irreparable harm in their name.

"You're not responsible for every endangered or displaced animal in the world, and that includes the human variety."

"I don't regret fighting for the horses or winning." Gunny turned her back on the horses and looked toward the path they'd come from, the path that led back to the soon-to-be-demolished foster home. "I just need to figure out how to save those kids now."

"I don't know Savy very well, but I get the sense she's going to figure out a way to protect those children. Maybe let her handle it?"

Gunny shook her head, the wheels in her brain already turning over possibilities. "I move quicker on my own."

"You sound like a sniper." Truman grinned. "Without a gun. You just have your words and your will. You could probably topple a whole government with just those two weapons."

Gunny was too busy with her own thoughts. That had to be why she missed the oncoming assault. Truman's hands cupped her cheek, one on each side. His palms were softer than she would've expected for so physical a man. Just like the memory foam soft-firmness of his chest, the flesh of his hands was a cushion that conformed to the contours of her face.

She wanted to rest in his hold. To fall asleep and leave all her cares and worries to the setting sun. No, that wasn't the sun setting. It was her eyelashes sinking downward as she allowed herself to relax in his embrace.

"Gunny?"

"Hmmm?"

"I'm going to kiss you."

Her eyes blinked open. Gun-metal gray was all she could see. Gray had always been a cold, dreary color in Gunny's mind. Until she saw the heat in Truman's gaze.

"Why?" She had to clear the huskiness from her throat and try again. "Why are you going to kiss me?"

"A man and woman—husband and wife, actually. Out alone in the woods. Seems like what should naturally happen. Don't you think?"

"I... I..." Gunny was supposed to say no. Problem was, she'd have to close her mouth to make that sound, and her lips refused to back down and make the motion.

It had to be the shame, or the guilt, or the stress of the day. Why else would she be eager to have this man's lips pressed against hers? She didn't even like him.

Except she knew she wouldn't still be on her feet without him at her side. She was only standing because he'd kept a hand on her back. He'd had an arm wrapped around her shoulders. Now his fingers were warm against her skin.

He was right. It did seem like the most natural thing to have happen right now. Truman's head came toward hers slowly, allowing her to make a run for it if she wanted.

For the first time in a long time, Gunny Silver held still. Once again, she felt certain that Truman felt familiar. His mouth against hers was more than a memory. It was a plan, an outline for a future that was hers for the taking.

Her fingers dug into his shoulders as though in protest of past separation. Her chest pressed against his, resisting any attempt of air to come between them. Her breath was the signature that sealed the deal that she was in this for the long battle.

CHAPTER FIFTEEN

Truman's senses were on high alert. That was typically the way when he was staking out a spot. The world would slow down so that he could pick out every minute detail.

He smelled the ripe berries on the breeze from the east.

He felt every fist-size rock under his shoe, which he kicked aside to have a level playing field.

He heard the melodic chirp of every bird, the busy rustling of every bug.

His gaze filled with sunlight, blonde rays of light shining brighter and brighter as each strand came to set around tan shoulders while the sun overhead began its slow descent toward the horizon.

All that was left was to taste.

Truman's trigger finger was on Gunnery Silver's chin. No, not Gunnery Silver. She was Gunnery Bates.

She was his. He'd tracked his quarry. He'd acquired his target. Now he had her surrounded. He just needed to pull the trigger.

He brushed his lower lip against hers. The shuddery breath she let out nearly made him blow his cover. That cover being that this marriage was fake. That cover being that he would let her get on a plane in a couple of days. That cover being he didn't want to possess this woman with the whole of his being.

With a groan, Truman covered her mouth with his. He couldn't be silent in his attack. He couldn't be stealth in making this advance. Truman wanted this woman too much. He wanted to come out of the shadows and proclaim that he needed her. That he never wanted to be apart from her. He felt himself attaching to Gunny like he was now her shadow.

He pulled her closer, deepening the kiss. He expected a fight from this firebrand of a woman. She put up no defense. Instead, Gunnery Silver Bates gave in.

Her hands rested against his chest. Her fingers

snaked around his neck and into his hair. Then she tugged, pulling him closer as though she couldn't get enough of him.

Truman understood the sentiment. He couldn't get close enough. He couldn't get enough, period.

The rock under Truman's foot ground into pebbles as it cracked under the added weight of having Gunny in his arms. The berries smelled overripe next to the sweetness of Gunny's breath. The birdsong became noise next to the small gasps that Gunny made with each new kiss. Truman's eyes were closed tight in an effort to give him some reprieve from the onslaught of sensory overload. Even still, behind his closed eyelids, all he could see was a bright light.

His every instinct told him to go into that light. If death was on the other side, he'd die a happy man and thank his Maker for those few moments of bliss with that angel.

A new sound penetrating. This rustling was heavier than a bug. It was too loud to be an insect or a small mammal. This was something bigger.

Truman did not want to stop kissing Gunny. The soldier in him urged him to pay attention. It was more important than anything that she was safe.

That thought alerted Truman to the fact that there was a threat at his back.

He pulled away from her, just enough to allow a breeze of air between them. Even that half an inch was too much. A war for his attention broke out in his head.

Truman knew he should look up and assess the danger he was sensing. But he couldn't turn his gaze away from Gunny. Her head remained tilted, waiting for the next kiss. It took everything in Truman to turn away from those lush lips and seek out the potential threat.

Please let it be a bunny hopping by, he thought to himself. *Or a curious deer that posed no threat.*

When Truman turned his head, he did see fur. Unfortunately, it was not the soft white fur of a bunny rabbit. It was not the gangly four legs of a deer. What Truman saw was a large, dark creature eying them curiously. Its paws were the size of his head. It's black fur bristled.

The bear took a step forward. Truman knew better than to make any sudden movements. He avoided eye contact, which was hard when he wanted to proclaim his dominance in this situation. There would be nothing that could stand between him and protecting Gunny.

He knew they had to walk away slowly. He knew he couldn't scream or yell. Laying down and curling his body into a ball felt like an anathema, but he would do it if it would protect his wife.

Truman reached out to Gunny to begin their descent to the ground. Only Gunny had pulled away from him. Truman turned his head slowly to let her know what they were up against. When he turned, he heard a click and was met with the barrel of his own gun.

Somehow Gunny had managed to get the gun and clip from his waistband and pocket. She held the weapon out, aimed squarely at the bear. There were tears in her eyes, but her hand was steady.

Her lips were moving. Just slightly. The whispered words were shaky as they left her mouth.

"Please, go. Please, go. Don't make me do this."

Truman had pulled the trigger of a gun many times in his life. There was a silence each time, a certainty that came after. He'd been following orders each time, orders he believed in and would die for.

This standoff was against everything his wife held dear. She held a weapon in her hand. It was trained on an animal she likely had fought to protect.

Truman could not let her take this shot.

Behind him, he heard more rustling. Curling into a ball was no longer an option. Neither was looking away. Truman dared to turn around.

The bear had turned. It was moving away from them. Its paws crunching into rocks and silencing the birds overhead and bugs below.

The gun wobbled in Gunny's hand. For the second time since he met her, Truman stripped a weapon from Gunny's hands. This time when he did, she didn't cock her hands on her hips. She shook from the impact of what she'd almost done.

Part of him wondered if he should be upset that she hadn't batted an eyelash when she'd aimed the gun at him. But Truman knew that Gunny would've never put a bullet in him. Though she had been prepared to put a bullet in that bear if it had attacked. To kill an animal would've hurt her on a soul-deep level.

Truman pulled Gunny to him. She said nothing as she came into his embrace. He kept his arms wrapped around her as they walked back down the trail. He kept a lookout for more danger. All the while, he remained her shadow. Intent he would never let this woman out of his sight.

CHAPTER SIXTEEN

Gunny let Truman deposit her into the truck. He might have even carried her there. She wasn't sure. Her legs were shakier than a fawn taking its first steps.

Faintly, she heard the raised voices. The running of small feet against creaky hardwoods. Savy's melodic voice pressing for calm and order within Bright Horizons.

The click of metal against metal made her jump in her seat. The thick strap of the seatbelt kept her in place. That leather strap let her know that she was inside the cab of a truck and not back out in the wilderness facing off against a bear.

She'd been prepared to pull that trigger. She'd been a second away from doing so. For all her time spent standing up against armed hunters and poachers, Gunny had never once taken a gun and aimed it at another living thing. She'd never even considered it a possibility.

Until the bear had interrupted her make-out session with this man.

Truman's hands were at her midsection. His knuckles brushed against the fabric covering her belly button as he snapped the seatbelt into place. For some unknown reason, Gunny didn't feel trapped by the strap. She felt safe, secure, tethered where she had been tossing and turning.

When she looked up, she looked directly into his gaze. There were so many questions there. Questions she wasn't ready to answer.

Questions like, was she okay?

She had no idea if she was okay or not. Her mind was so full thinking about others. There was Father Matthews, who they still had no news from. There was Savy and the foster kids. There was the bear whose life she'd nearly ended.

Questions like, would she really have pulled that trigger?

Gunny still felt the cold steel of the gun in her palm. Her index finger had been on the trigger. Her entire body had shook, but not her trigger finger. That had been steady.

Truman brushed her hair out of her face, but he didn't say anything. He let her have her silence. The passenger side door slammed, shutting out the rest of the world. For the first time in her life, Gunny felt alone.

Solitude was a strange, foreign feeling for a twin. Stranger even for the sibling of a big family. Through all her travels across the world, Gunny had never felt alone.

The driver's side door of the truck opened, letting in a breath of fresh air. On the currents of that slight wind came the scent of turned earth, gunpowder, and the spicy scent that belonged to Truman.

The door shut and out went the feeling of solitude.

Truman slanted Gunny a look. It wasn't a smile. It wasn't a frown. It was simply a brush of his gaze over her face. When he was done, he gave her a slight nod as though she'd given him the answer to a question. Then he started the engine.

Gunny sat face forward as Truman pulled out of the foster home's drive and onto the main road. They drove in silence. The radio wasn't on. The windows weren't down for the breeze to intrude. All she could hear was the even breathing coming from his mouth.

She'd kissed that mouth. It had been an amazing kiss. The best of her life. Not that she'd had much practice to begin with. Clearly, Truman had.

Any man who could kiss like that—so thoroughly that they didn't hear the danger approaching them out in the woods. So passionately that she'd been prepared to kill when they'd been interrupted. Well, that was some skill.

"I'd rather not leave you alone tonight."

Gunny turned away from the sound of his voice. She couldn't let him see how her cheeks heated at not just the sound of his voice but those words. They had every right to spend the night together. They were married, man and wife.

"I hope you're not expecting your husbandly rights," she said.

From the corner of her eye, she caught the small smile that tugged at his lips. Truman's smiles were always small, as though they were hard-fought. She felt a slight thrill race over her skin that she'd won a few.

"You've been through a lot today," he said, gaze

still on the road. "Marriage to me. The ER. The foster home. And then there was the bear."

"Yeah," Gunny agreed, "that wedding was the most trying part of the day."

Again, she got another smile. This one a little bigger than the last. Truman looked over at her, and her breath caught.

She knew she looked a fright. She was still in her wedding dress, but it was no longer white. Her makeup had melted off under the day's sun. Her hair had come undone during either the march to City Hall or the trek through the woods of Clearwater Valley.

This is what life with her would be like. Gunny was always getting into a mess. It was always on purpose. Because it was often messy to save others. Gunny had no desire to live a pristine life.

"I am your husband," Truman said. "But I have no expectations of that role tonight. Other than to look after you."

"I'm not domesticated."

"I'm pretty feral myself."

"I can't stand still for long."

"There we differ," he said. "I can lay still for hours, days."

"While you wait for the perfect shot?"

"Yes." There was no apology in his voice. "I'm a very patient man. I know how to line up the perfect shot, and I never miss."

It didn't sound like he was bragging. It sounded cautionary, like he was warning her of an oncoming storm. Here she sat in the calm of the eye as they ambled down a country road.

"I don't need looking after," she said.

Truman pumped the brakes. With a flick of his wrist, he pulled the truck over to the side of the road. He placed the vehicle in park but left the engine running. Once all that was settled, he turned and faced her.

"I see you," he said.

Gunny jerked back as though he'd struck her. In a way, he had. Truman's steel gaze was like a bullet right to the chest. She felt her heart explode under the assault. The funny thing was, she didn't feel in pieces. She felt whole.

"I see you," he repeated. "And I'm pretty sure I can hold on to you."

Gunny was great at arguing. Before she'd become an activist, she'd been on the high school debate team. Other school teams would groan when she took the podium. But right now, in this moment, she couldn't craft any manner of argument. Only one word managed to escape her mouth.

"Why?"

"We're already married," he said. "So why not?"

That was not the answer. She could tell by looking at the twinkle in that gray gaze. The gaze she'd once thought was cold and unfeeling was anything but. Truman's eyes shone brightly at her, letting her see all his secrets and pressing into some of her own.

"You need someone watching your back," he said, leaning over the middle console.

He was close enough for a kiss. Gunny pressed her lips together, as though she could will them to not want what every part of her—her heart, her mind, even her soul—wanted from this man. Her body betrayed her as she let out a gasp of air.

Truman was going to kiss her again. There was nothing she could do about it. Not if she was at war inside herself. Only it wasn't a war. There was no line in the sand inside of her. Every part in her stood to one side. It was the side of the starting line of the race. All that was left was for someone to shout, Go!

No one said go. Neither of them said anything. They simply leaned into each other, meeting halfway until their lips touched.

She could have this. She could have him. Even if only for a little time. Or maybe a little while longer if she took an extended vacation at home. Or maybe even after that if she could convince her husband to come with her to Australia.

He'd made promises in those vows. Promises to grow with her, promises to face challenges, promises to open his heart. He'd scoffed at first as the vows were read, but by the end, she'd seen the shift in him. He'd started taking them seriously.

What if he was serious about them? He sure was kissing her like he had no plans to let her go anytime soon. Gunny was giving as good as she got. What if she had no plans to let him go anytime soon?

They didn't need to let go. They were man and wife. Father Matthews had proclaimed them so.

Gunny pulled back. Her whole body, along with Truman, protested the disconnection. "Wait!"

"What?" he said as he reached for her.

"He never said it."

"Who never said what?"

"Father Matthews. He never proclaimed us man and wife. Does that mean we're not married?"

CHAPTER SEVENTEEN

Stars were poking out of the dark sky when Truman pulled up to the hospital for the second time today. The tiny pinpricks of light shone down and settled on Gunny's face. She looked like an angel of the night, even with the smudges of dirt on her face, her unraveled hair, and the stains on her white dress.

There was a strong possibility that she wasn't his.

Even before the entire thought formed in his mind, he rejected it. The unspoken vows meant nothing. He didn't need to have an official make the proclamation. Truman knew with every fiber of his being that this woman was meant to be in his arms, by his side, for the rest of his days.

The real question was, would she make the same vow to him?

Gunny stumbled as she walked beside him. Truman reached out to her, wrapping an arm around her waist and bringing her into the protection of his body. She came without protest, as though they'd been walking side by side for years. As though they would continue to do so for years to come.

No matter what Father Matthews had or hadn't said, they were a unit. They would remain a unit. It didn't matter if they were legally married or not.

Only it did. Because this was the last day to meet the deadline of General Silver's will. If their union wasn't legal, the family, his unit, they would all lose everything. Worst of all, Gunny would have no reason to stay.

For now, Gunny let him hold her hand as they walked through the hospital. He rubbed at her index finger. The same finger that had rested on the trigger of a gun. The same finger that had been prepared to end the life of an animal if it had charged him.

She felt something for him. The least of which was indifference. So why was she tugging her hand away from him and running to another man?

"Charlie!" Gunny called as she flung herself into a dark-haired man's hold.

"Hey, Gunny Bunny," said the man as his arms wrapped around Truman's wife.

Or possibly his not-wife. Even if Gunny wasn't his legal wife, she was still entirely his. Even if she had yet to fling herself into Truman's arms.

"What happened to you?" asked Charlie, looking her up and down. "You look like you fought a bear."

"Not too far from the truth. I was at Bright Horizon's talking with Savy and—"

Charlie straightened as though a lightning rod had zipped up his spine. "Savy? How is she? Is she okay? She didn't do this to you… did she?"

"No, we… It's a long story." Gunny sighed, placing her hands on either side of Charlie's face. "I'm so sorry about your dad."

Charlie closed his eyes and rested his forehead against Gunny's. "He's stable. The doctors say he's going to be okay. He just needs to wake up."

They were talking about Father Matthews. Truman searched the man's face for any resemblance between the two men. He couldn't find a single one in Charlie Matthews's tan skin and angular nose.

The other man must have felt Truman's stare. He

looked up, his arms still wrapped around Gunny. "I'm sorry? Are we blocking your way?"

Truman grit his teeth and prayed for calm. Other than the familiarity the man had with his wife, or possibly not-wife, there was no reason to gut him. Not when his father was lying ill in a hospital bed.

But Truman couldn't stop glaring at the hand Charlie Matthews had at Gunny's hip. Until he saw the plastic ring on his hand. It looked like it came out of a Cracker Jack box. It was the second of its kind Truman had seen today.

"Charlie, this is Truman," said Gunny. "He's my…"

"I'm her husband," said Truman.

"Well, we don't know that for sure," said Gunny.

Truman knew it for sure. Gunny was his. It didn't matter if another man had declared it or not. It was simply a fact.

"They told me he was performing a wedding when this happened," said Charlie. "It was your ceremony?"

Gunny nodded. Guilt clouding her blue gaze. She crossed her arms over her chest and rubbed her forearms as though seeking comfort. She couldn't think this was her fault? Could she?

Truman took a step to bring her into the comfort of his arms. Charlie Matthews got there first.

"It's not your fault, Gunny Bunny," Charlie soothed. "If it's anybody's fault, it's his sons. We left him there to do all that work by himself."

It was a touching moment. Truly, it was. The boy next door comforting the girl next door. Except the female neighbor in question belonged in Truman's arms.

"He didn't finish the ceremony," Gunny said, stepping out of Charlie's arms. "He never pronounced us man and wife."

Behind him, Truman heard Scout curse. He turned to find Scout, Linc, and the rest of the Silver sisters and President's Men coming from what looked like the hospital cafeteria.

Charlie looked past Gunny to Truman. His gaze was one part quizzical, one part assessment. Not as though he was sizing up a rival. More of an appraisal of his worth to date this particular Silver sister. That's when Truman saw the resemblance to Father Matthews.

Charlie Matthews was just as protective of the Silvers as his father. Truman straightened his own spine to show he was strong enough for Gunny. He stepped forward, standing shoulder to shoulder with his wife to indicate that they were a unit, vows or not.

"It's okay," said Charlie. "When he wakes up, I'm sure he'll be more than happy to do it."

"We don't have that much time," said Gunny. "My father's deadline for us all to get married so that we could keep the ranch was today."

Charlie gave a shake of his head, but confusion still marred his brow when he focused on Gunny. "Exactly what did I miss while I was away?"

"You're a preacher's son," Gunny said, ignoring his question. "We had a ceremony, so that makes us married. Right?"

"It's not the ceremony that makes you legally married," said Charlie. "It's the paperwork. Once you file the marriage license, that's when you're actually married."

"Where's the license?" Gunny turned to face her family.

"Father Matthews took care of it with each of our weddings," said Scout. "It's probably with his things."

"I'll go ask about his personal effects," said Charlie as he took off down the hall.

But as Charlie disappeared around the corner, another voice spoke up. "I have them."

It was the second time today that an enemy had snuck up on Truman. Now his pulse sped up to triple time. He felt the heat of a target on his back. Instinctively, he pulled Gunny into the circle of his arms. He didn't miss that each man of his unit did the same to his own wife as Catherine walked toward them.

Her stilettos impacted the parquet floor like bullets firing from an automatic rifle. Each impact reverberated through Truman's head. He itched for a weapon to protect himself, to protect Gunny, to protect their family. All the while, he knew there was none.

Catherine held in her hands the only thing that would've protected them all from her. The single sheet of paper crinkled in her painted claws. Because she held Truman and Gunny's unfiled marriage license.

CHAPTER EIGHTEEN

Gunny stared at the sheath of paper in her stepmother's hands. She'd often stared in fascination at Catherine's hands. Her nails were always impeccable. Perfectly rounded points with a pale color that always matched her outfit and makeup to perfection. Gunny's nails always matched her clothing and what was on her face as well. Because what was always on her clothes, her face, and under her nails was dirt.

Today was no different. She stood in her wedding dress that was now artfully decorated with grass stains from when she'd knelt beside Father Matthews at her ceremony. There was dust from when she'd stormed into the City Hall. There were spats of dry dirt from her trek into the woods.

"It's too late for you to file it today. The court-house closed over an hour ago," Catherine continued. "Which means that you girls didn't meet your dear dad's requirements. So, the ranch goes to me."

The air conditioner clicked on overhead. The chilly gust blew down on them, causing the stiff sheet of paper to bend downward. It made a crinkling sound as though the fibers were about to crack under the pressure of remaining in Catherine's grasp.

"Mother, you don't want to do this." Mareen stepped to the front of the lines, Wilson close on her heels.

"I didn't do anything," said Catherine. "I've only sat by and watched this all play out just as I told you it would."

"We all did what our dad wanted," said Scout. "As twisted as it was. It worked out for all of us. We all found love."

Catherine cocked her head as she took in Scout and Linc. Linc wrapped Scout up in his arms, smiling down at her with complete adoration in his eyes. Catherine's gaze lighted on each of the couples. Jefferson had one arm wrapped around Saylor, his lips resting against her temple, which was scrunched in worry. Jackson leaned heavily on a cane with one hand, but the other was wrapped tight around Brig, who clutched at the fabric of his shirt. Tilly and Carter were wrapped around one another like they were one heart beating.

"Not all of you," said Catherine, her gaze landing on Truman and Gunny.

When Gunny looked up at Truman, her heart beat steady. Not missing a single beat. Truman didn't wrap his arms around her as though they were madly in love. Because they weren't. They weren't even married.

But he never left her side. He kept his hand at her back, a steady presence letting her know she would not face this alone.

"We did what our father wanted," said Scout. "You can't swoop in on your broomstick on a technicality."

"There are no participation trophies in life," said Catherine. "You either win, or you lose."

"You're wrong, mother," said Mareen. "You're about to lose if you do this."

"I've tried to tell you that there are no happily ever afters. That's not the way the world works."

"I'm pregnant." Mareen place her hands over her still flat belly.

Catherine's stony face went impossibly still. She

didn't blink. She didn't breathe. She only stared at her daughter's midsection.

"If you take away the ranch, if you take away your grandbaby's home… I don't think I could ever forgive you. That ranch is where all my best memories are. It's the place where we will always belong. That ranch is where our family is."

With that word *family*, Catherine blinked. It was as though any emotion she'd been trying to hide was leeched from her porcelain features. "That ranch is a money suck."

"Is not," Scout said, taking a step forward. Linc held her back.

"Despite what you girls think," said Catherine, "I am doing this for your future. I'll sell the land and reinvest the money. That is true security for your futures when these fake marriages all fail."

Gunny expected each one of her sisters to shout. For at least one of them to stomp her feet. For all of them to deny Catherine's words about anything fake.

No one spoke up. They all looked at the older woman as though she were a child who could not be reasoned with.

Catherine held out the marriage license to

Gunny. Her pale pink nails were a compliment to the sepia tone document. Both her and Truman's names were printed with a swirl of dark black lettering. The name of the document was embossed in gold.

It looked official, even though it meant nothing outside of the filing cabinet of the courthouse. What was karma up to with her? One document she had filed years ago, and it came back around today to wreak havoc on a family. Another document she needed filed an hour ago, and because it hadn't been, it would wreak havoc on her family.

"Do you still want it?" Catherine said, her red-coated lips curling as she spoke. "Not that it matters."

Gunny's gaze fixated on Catherine's lips. A poisoned red apple came to mind. Though Catherine looked nothing like an old crone in a black cloak, and they weren't out in the woods. Still, Gunny felt certain this had to be some kind of trick.

If she reached for the proffered prize would it turn into a snake and bite her? Sending poison through her veins that would settle her down for a long, motionless sleep that made her entirely depen-dent on a long-awaited prince? If she didn't reach for the fancy piece of paper, would she be the only one unscathed by the witch's spell, free to continue on her quest to save the world?

Gunny didn't have to decide. Truman took the document from Catherine's hands. There was a sharp protest at the exchange of hands. Gunny's heart stopped at the thought the paper would rip. Then there would be nothing—real or fake— holding her and Truman together.

Was that what she wanted? They had lost this battle. Her third loss of the day behind Father Matthews's heart attack, Savy losing the foster home, and now this; her marriage wisping away like a fanciful little girl's dream.

The sheet of paper straightened and went silent in Truman's hold. He didn't crumple into a heap at the touch of the document. His eyes didn't close as he fell into a deep slumber. He remained alert and vigilant as ever. He reached out his free hand and settled it again at Gunny's low back.

Gunny felt entirely awake at his warm touch. She felt like no harm could befall her. Not from a poisoned piece of fruit, a wicked witch, or even her stepmother.

However, that wasn't the case for the rest of her family. Behind her, Gunny heard the shaky sighs of defeat at Catherine's words. She saw the winces in the eyes of her sisters. She watched as each of their husbands helplessly pulled their wives to their chests, as though their bravery might still save them, might still save the ranch.

CHAPTER NINETEEN

Truman should be car sick with how many times he'd been in a vehicle today. For a man who was used to trekking through all forms of terrain and then lying low for hours, even days on end, it was more movement that he'd had to manage in over a year. His body did ache. But not because of the fourth car ride of the day.

His world was off its kilter.

He wasn't married. In his heart, yes. Legally, not at all.

That was any easy fix. They would simply file the paperwork in the morning. The real trouble was the fate of the ranch.

They pulled into the gates of the sprawling

homestead well into the dead of the night. Scout and Linc had stayed behind with Charlie Matthews to be with Father Matthews in case he woke up. They wanted to be sure the old man had family around when he opened his eyes.

A few lights were on in the main house when Truman put the truck in park. He was dirty and sweaty and tired, but the day was far from over for him. He turned to look at Gunny in the passenger seat.

She looked like a fallen angel to him. Not fallen due to any deeds, just the dust that settled about her halo of blonde hair, the smudges on her white dress, and the scuffs on her shoes. In her lap sat the marriage license. She ran her thumb over the B on his last name.

"We should talk," he said.

Gunny startled. She glanced up at him as though she had forgotten he was there. There was a cloud hovering in the depths of her blue eyes. Truman smelled an oncoming storm.

"There's no need," she said, placing the license on the dashboard of the car. "I need to get packing."

She reached for the handle and hopped out of the truck. Truman was so stunned by her words that it took him a precious second to move into action. He was out of the truck and around to her before she'd taken more than two steps.

"Packing?"

Again, those blue eyes glanced up at him as though she'd already forgotten his very presence. "Yes, I need to pack. I think I can move my flight up a few days. I don't have many of my belongings here, so they won't need my help to pack up my cabin."

"You're leaving?"

"Yes," she said, stepping around him.

Truman took two more steps, which was enough to bring him back into her direct line. Gunny stopped in her tracks and looked up at him. Now that he was there, words escaped him.

He didn't need her to repeat herself. He'd heard her clearly. She was going to pack. Going to pack to leave him.

He didn't need clarification that she was going on a weekend vacation. She was leaving the country. Going somewhere in the Outback, and because she wouldn't have this place to come home to, he might never see her again.

"What?"

The word was a whisper that rattled on her

tongue before it came out. That single word impacted him right in the chest. It pierced his heart, like his chest was a target, and she'd hit her mark.

"What?" she asked again, her voice growing louder, more firm.

He couldn't find any words. He was out in the open. There was no cover for him.

When she shook her head and went to step around him, Truman's arm shot out to catch her. His right arm. There was no pain when he lifted his arm.

"What do you think you're doing?" Gunny said as she looked at his fingers grasping her arm.

Those were the first words she'd ever said to him. It had been right after she'd kicked his weapon out of his hold. His shoulder had ached then. It didn't ache now.

"Truman, let me go. It's over."

"No."

"No, what?"

"No," he said, "this is not going to happen."

They were having a repeat conversation from the first time they met. Truman was determined this would not be the last time they spoke.

"We're fighters, you and I," he insisted, pulling her close. "We're not giving up."

"We've lost," she said, pulling away from him. "It's time to move on."

"Is that what you're going to tell Savy and those kids?"

Her back went ramrod straight.

"What about Father Matthews when he wakes up. Or your sisters when they have to pack up their whole lives."

"This isn't your life," she said. "This isn't even your fight. You were going to be out of here soon after me. This is just a house. My sisters will find new homes. So will Savy and those kids. But there are animals out there who are just going to die. At least I can do something about that."

"What about us?"

"There is no us. You're free to go and do whatever you were going to do."

The ache grew in his shoulder, allowing her to pull away from him easily. For the first time in his life, he'd taken a shot. And he'd missed.

"I see it now," he said. "This is what you do. This is your pattern."

"What pattern?"

"You start a fight, and then you leave."

Her shoulders jerked. He hadn't missed the shot

this time. Unfortunately, Gunny stayed true to her pattern.

She took a step back, preparing to walk away from this battle. Truman mirrored her, mimicking the retreat. Gunny stepped back until she was at the door to the main house. Truman backed away from her until he blended into the shadows.

CHAPTER TWENTY

"*O*oof."

Gunny came awake from a heel to the back of her head. She and her twin had been laying head to foot in their stepmom's old bed. Though they'd never called Sarah Silver stepmom. Because she had been the only mother the twins had ever known.

All of her sisters had piled into their mom's old bed last night. They'd huddled together as they did when one of them was sick, or upset, or simply because it was a random Tuesday, and they'd stayed up all night gabbing and fussing and fighting and loving each other in that way that no one who wasn't a Silver would understand.

Gunny disentangled herself from the arm Saylor

had slung over her midsection. Her older sister curled her fingers into Gunny's dress—the white sundress she'd worn at her wedding nearly twenty-four hours ago. One by one, Gunny unfurled Saylor's fingers until the slumbering woman let her go.

Next, Gunny had to climb over Scout, who was spread out like a starfish at the edge of the bed. Scout wasn't so much hogging the mattress as she had a hand or a toe reaching out to touch each of her sisters. That was Scout's way; she had to have her hand in each of her sister's lives.

Brig had opted for the old rocking chair near the window. The baby of the family had always striven to strike out on her own. But in her independence, Brig was always close by her sisters.

Mareen lay curled in a fetal position in the center of the bed, her hands protecting her belly. A new generation of Silvers would be here in less than a year. But the new kids on the block wouldn't have a field of honeysuckles to run in. They wouldn't get to see wild horses run at the edge of their property.

Of course, her sisters intended to fight their stepmother's claim to the ranch. They were Silvers, after all.

Gunny stood at the door of their mother's

bedroom door. She looked out at her sisters sleeping peacefully in the knowledge that even though they'd lost the battle, they were gearing up for a war. A war they intended to win with the only weapon being their unity.

The space on the bed where Gunny had slept still held the shape of her body. She'd only fallen asleep a few hours ago, and her body was still tired from all the stress of the previous day. A part of her ached to go settle back in that spot where she knew she was safe and surrounded. But the itch that had always been inside of her agitated the bottom of her bare feet. She needed to get moving.

Moving where, she wasn't sure? Hopping on a plane and flying halfway around the world did not sound appealing. But neither did standing still. She just wasn't sure which way to turn?

"You looking for Truman?"

Gunny looked up to see Linc with a steamy mug of coffee in one hand and a pad of Post-it notes in the other. She set her lips to say the word No but choked on the response.

Truman was the last person she wanted to see. He'd accused her of being a turn tail last night. She wasn't a runner. She was a fighter.

That was her whole business model. She'd swoop

in, show the locals how to fight the power, then she'd be off to the next fight. That wasn't running. It was delegating. There were so many fights, and she couldn't be everywhere at once.

"He went out to get some target practice in before we head out to look at some other properties."

"Other properties?" said Gunny.

"We're making contingencies for a Plan B," said Lincoln. "In case we can't win the deed back from your stepmother."

Can't win? Gunny knew this was going to be a battle, but she'd never considered losing it. What if Catherine actually made good on her threat of selling the ranch? What if she could never come back to this place again?

Even worse, if this place wasn't here, then she might never see Truman again. They weren't legally married. He had no reason to stay. After last night, she wouldn't be surprised if he was already planning to leave.

Gunny's mind was a whirl. She didn't want to never see Truman again. But she didn't want to stay put. She didn't want to give up this ranch. But could she stay and fight the long-drawn-out war with her sisters?

Shame rolled over her that that was even a question in her mind. Already she'd caused a mess with Bright Horizons and the wild horses of Clearwater Valley. Was she truly going to leave Savy and those kids to blow in the wind?

No. No, she was going to stay and fight this out until the end. But first, she was going to find her husband and tell him that. He needed to know that he was wrong. That would be the first fight she'd win today.

CHAPTER TWENTY-ONE

Truman couldn't sleep. The silence on the ranch had been deafening last night. Even now, in the bright light of a new day, the animals seemed to know there was something wrong.

The horses were restless in the pen. Birds were quiet up in the trees. So too were the insects. Either an earthquake or storm was coming. Or the animals knew the wicked witch would be flying in soon on her broomstick.

Truman chided himself for that uncharitable thought. The girls might call Catherine evil, but he'd seen the look in her eyes when Mareen announced she was pregnant. That was the look only a mother would give to her child when she wanted to reach out.

They might lose the ranch, but Truman knew that his brothers and their wives would never fall out of touch. The only if in that equation was his wife. Because despite the unfiled paperwork, Gunny was his.

He'd come to this ranch wanting nothing more than to fulfill the dying wish of his commander and help his daughters. All while rehabilitating his shoulder to get back into active duty. Now the only duty Truman wanted to act on was fighting to get Gunny to stay in his arms.

He was a master of disguise. He could hide in plain sight and watch over her every move. He was prepared to follow her to the ends of the earth.

Gunny might have a habit of starting a fight and leaving. But Truman had a habit of stalking his quarry and never missing a shot. He wasn't about to let his wife ruin his perfect record.

He lay on his belly out at the edge of the property. The target was within his scope, not that he needed to magnify the bull's eye. He spied the yellow center of the bull's eye. Then a flash of white came into his sight.

Truman blinked, trying to clear his vision. But

even after he wiped at his eyes, the apparition didn't dissipate.

Gunny stood in front of his target. She was still dressed in the white dress she'd worn for their wedding. Though calling it white was a stretch as the garment had picked up even more dirt and dust from her trek out to this part of the property.

"Don't shoot," she said.

Truman was already laying his weapon down and clamoring to his feet. He'd been prepared to hunt her down. To stalk her. But there she stood. With her hands raised in the air in the universal sign of surrender.

He closed the distance between them and was on her in a heartbeat. Truman scooped Gunny up into his arms. His shoulder protested the move, but he ignored the ache. The one in his heart had his full attention.

"Hey," she said from inside the cradle of his arms.

"Hey," he mimicked, tightening his hold.

She wasn't squirming to get away. In fact, she was holding entirely still. Likely because of the way he was holding her, her feet dangled off the ground.

He didn't set her down. He wasn't taking any chances of her getting away now that he'd caught her.

"I'm supposed to get on a flight tomorrow," she said.

"I know." Truman was already in the process of booking his own flight to Australia. He wasn't entirely sure of Gunny's itinerary. But he had no doubts of his tracking skills. He would find her wherever she went.

Although maybe now that he held her captive, he could simply ask her where she'd be.

"I was thinking I should postpone the trip, though." She avoided his gaze. Her fingers played with the collar of his shirt. Still, she made no move to get away from him. "There are things left unfinished here that I feel I should attend to."

"Things?"

She nodded, now playing with the top button of his shirt. "The foster home, for one. I can't just leave Savy to deal with that on her own. Not when I started the fight."

"I'm sure Savy and those kids would appreciate your help and expertise in that matter. Is that all?"

"Then there's Father Matthews. He's going to need some help when he gets out of the hospital."

"Is there any other matter you want resolved before you leave, Gunnery?"

Gunny's blue gaze finally lifted and caught his. "There's the matter of us."

"Us?"

"We should probably figure out… you know, our legal standing. Since we're not technically married."

Truman spanned his hands over her back, pressing her closer to him. His shoulder had stopped protesting long ago. He wanted to carry this particular load for the rest of his life.

"We made vows to each other," he said. "We pledged to develop our hearts and minds together. I don't see what the law has to do with any of that."

"You still want to… do all of that?"

"I'm already doing it," he said. "My heart is yours. Whether you want it or not. You get on that plane, I'll be in the aisle seat beside you."

"I hate the window seat," she said.

"Fine, then you take the aisle. I'll just have to deal with being trapped on an eighteen-hour flight."

"You were going to come with me?" she asked.

"Yes. Right after I took the marriage license to the courthouse. I want the right to stand by your side, even if you wanted to get rid of me."

"I don't want to get rid of you."

"You were never in any danger of that." He pulled

her to him. "I'm in love with you, Gunnery Silver Bates."

"Technically, it's still Gunnery Silver."

"Not for long."

Truman set Gunny down on the ground. He had to if he was going to keep his balance and ravage her mouth at the same time. The moment his lips touched hers, he knew he'd made the right decision because his knees wobbled with the impact.

The taste of her upper lip was like the fire from a gunshot. Her lower lip set off detonations inside his head that would rival the Fourth of July. When he deepened the kiss, his entire body jerked like the kickback of his rifle. Only there was no pain, no ache anywhere in his person. He wanted more. Now he knew he was going to have as much as he ever wanted because she was his. She had surrendered to him long after he'd surrendered to her.

"I love you too, Truman," she said. "I was going to fight for you. I just wasn't sure how to do it."

"You've already won me over," he said, brushing a kiss to her temple. "I'm pretty sure it was when you stripped my gun from me that first day."

She laughed, her lips spreading into a wide grin. Her eyes crinkling at the corners. It was the first time Truman had seen the expression. He was determined to have a repeat performance every day for the rest of their lives.

"We're going to win this fight for the ranch," she said when she sobered. Once again, a fierce warrior. "But after we do, I'm going to want to travel again and save more wild horses and endangered animals."

"I already had plans to stalk you. Now I don't have to be as stealthy. We'll face all these new battles together."

Gunny wrapped her arms around his neck. "I think I'm gonna like having you at my back."

"You'll have to fight me to keep me away from you," he said.

"This is a fight I'll be happy to let you win."

"*Let* me win?"

She grinned. Truman decided to give up this battle and claim another kiss from the woman who his heart had developed an unbreakable bond with. Later today, they'd go into town and make it legal. That would put an end to this particular fight and start them on their journey to forever.

EPILOGUE

*S*cout walked the length of the solicitor's office. The office wasn't on the main street of the small Montana town she'd lived all her life in. The town was only considered small due to its population. The square footage of Honor Valley could fit the island of Manhattan inside a couple of times. But the people could all fit into the high school football stadium with enough elbow room to be comfortable. Though they'd all likely be hugging each other while mixing and mingling.

In fact, in the dining room just down the hall, there was a good portion of the town's population. From this distance, Scout heard her sisters' high-pitched gabbing and their husbands' deep grumbling assent. Mixed in with the President's Men's low tones were voices she'd known for years. A couple of the Matthews boys had come home now that their father was out of the hospital, though not entirely back on his feet.

Scout's gaze went to the photographs on the wall. There were many crackled, sepia tone images of soldiers throughout history. From the Buffalo Soldiers and Tuskegee Airman of Haran Matthews's past. There was also a large framed picture of a young Father Matthews with his wife, Tessa. The couple was surrounded by six boys of varying skin tones. Each boy smiled a big toothsome grin as they hugged one of the adults or each other. Behind the patchwork family stood the Bright Horizon's Foster Home where the boys had spent the beginning years of their lives before the Matthews had adopted each one.

Father Matthews sat behind the ancient oak desk under which Scout had never been found in games of hide and seek. The old man's eyes were closed as they both waited. The lines that had been at the corners of his eyes and the dark circles that had been below had faded now that he'd had a few weeks of rest at home.

The man was itching to get back out in the field. It took all the Silver girls, all the President's Men, and half of the Matthews boys to keep him inside and seated, if not lying down in bed. Though Scout suspected he was sneaking out at night to walk the lands.

She couldn't blame him. She hated to be away from the land for long. If things went wrong today, she would no longer have any rights to walk Silver Star Ranch at any time of the day or night.

A sleek town car pulled into the drive. A pair of six-inch heels smacked down against the dirt. Catherine climbed out of the car, dressed in a pale pink dress that wouldn't last five seconds if she didn't get inside and out of the dust storm.

The wind kicked up, swirling a small cloud of dirt at her heels. Catherine lowered her sunshades and glared at the tiny tornado. The dirt dropped where it had risen. Thus confirming what Scout believed all along; that her stepmother was the Wicked Witch incarnate. She just drove a Bentley instead of a broomstick.

"I have a bad feeling about this," Scout muttered under her breath.

"Just give her a chance," said Father Matthews, his eyes still closed as though he was talking in his sleep. "She might surprise you."

Catherine came into the office. Her gaze didn't

go to Father Matthews, who now sat upright in his chair. Neither did it go to Scout, who stood at the opposite end of the room. Catherine's gaze landed on the picture on the wall. The old photograph featured a skinny Black man with his arm around a barrel-chested white man. Both men sported the modern camouflage style of military fatigues, handle-bar mustaches, and broad, toothsome grins that told the viewer that they were solemnly up to no good.

"Good afternoon, Catherine."

"Haran, how are you feeling today?" Catherine's gaze softened as she looked at Father Matthews.

"Ticker's still ticking. That's all I can ask for."

Catherine offered him a smile. Scout had to blink a couple of times at the warmth she saw there. Catherine was never warm.

As confirmed when her gaze landed on Scout. Her light gaze didn't exactly chill over, but it definitely dropped a few degrees.

"Let's get this over with, shall we," Catherine said, taking a seat.

"This won't take long at all," said Scout, taking the seat opposite her stepmother. "This is a check for the value of the ranch."

Each Silver sister and her husband had emptied

out their checking and savings account. They had gotten loans, pawned valuables, begged, and borrowed until they'd scrounged up enough money to outbid the highest buyer for the ranch.

Catherine looked down at the massive check Scout held in her hand and sniffed. "I'm not interested."

The words should've left Scout cold. Instead, she felt her skin overheating. The fingers holding the check with the obscene amount of zeros trembled in her hands as she glared at Catherine.

Father Matthews wore a serene smile, as though he had not a care in the world. Scout wondered if the doctors had messed with the old man's heart. This was the worst news in the world. What if Catherine was going to sell the ranch to a dude farm? Father Matthews would never have any peace with city slickers falling off horses at every turn.

"This offer is more than fair," said Scout. "Unless you're just being spiteful."

"What I am going to be is a grandmother." Catherine shuddered at that word. "Though I think I'll prefer to be called Grammy, like the solid gold statue. Yes, I think that would suit me more."

Scout could only stare in utter disbelief. Catherine was determining what Mareen's unborn child would call her while leaving that child homeless.

"However, I don't want my grandchild to run around my house with sticky fingers in that stocky form I know they'll get from that father of theirs. I have too many precious things in there that are breakable."

With Scout so busy staring, she didn't have enough brain cells to react when Catherine snatched the check out of her hand… and then tore it in half.

Scout gasped as the zeroes were split in half and then fluttered to the floor. "What the… how could… are you…?"

"I've decided the best investment will be if he or she be raised on the ranch," Catherine continued as though Scout hadn't spoken. "I've placed the deed in a family trust that is to be shared equally by Silver females."

Catherine took a document out of her expensive purse. The title at the top of the document did, in fact, read Deed. There was a lot of legal mumbo jumbo, but Scout knew what a premise of a deed was. It was the part that laid out the parties. In that part were the words Silver female descendants.

Scout's emotions vacillated from shock to disbelief. If she was understanding Catherine right, they weren't going to lose the ranch. Everything was set to rights, and they wouldn't have to leave their home. And wonder of wonders, there didn't appear to be a catch. No strings attached, like they had to turn over their firstborn children.

"Since I was once a Silver female," Catherine continued, "that means I still retain an equal share to the land."

Ah. Here was the catch.

"Which means I can come and go as I please… to see my grandchildren, mind you. I can't have the next generation being raised entirely feral."

That was it? Catherine just wanted the right to see her grandchild? Scout could've told her that all she'd ever need to do was knock on the door. Mareen would never keep her baby from her mother.

Over the last few months, Mareen had grown increasingly nostalgic about her times with her mother. Scout did wonder if some of the stories she told were confused due to baby brain. Though the woman who sat across from Scout now faintly resembled the doting mother of Mareen's imagination.

"On behalf of your daughter and stepdaughters, we accept. But you should know there will be more than one feral grandchild running around next year."

"Mareen's having twins?" Catherine looked to the door of the office where the low murmur of voices could still be heard.

"No, she's not. I'm pregnant, as well." Scout rested her hand over the small bump at her midsection. "So is Saylor and Tilly. Looks like you're getting four Grammy's."

"Wait? No. You're not my… I'm not your…"

Catherine couldn't complete the sentences. Because even through all the ups and downs of the years, the divorces and marriages, they were hers. She was theirs. They were family. And it was high time they started acting like it.

The grin on Father Matthews's face told Scout she had finally learned the lesson of the day. It always came down to family. Love them or leave them, but you could never break those bonds.

"Too late, Catherine," said Scout. "The paperwork is signed. You're a part of this family. In perpetuity according to this deed."

Catherine took a deep breath. Then she let it out slowly. Her regal shoulders went back. The glare she gave Scout didn't have the same bite that Scout remembered from her childhood.

"Fine," Catherine said.

"Fine," Scout said.

"Fine," Father Matthews chuckled. "Now that Abe's plan is complete, and all of his girls are cared for, I know he's resting in peace."

"You really think this is what he had planned all along?" asked Scout. "To get all of us together?"

Father Matthews shrugged. "Whatever he planned, it worked out for everyone. His daughters, his men, and his remaining wife are all taken care of on the land he loved. Who knows? I might even take a cue from my old friend when it comes to my boys."

The Silver sisters' stories are complete.
But the Matthews boys' stories are about to begin.
Only the Matthews boys can step in and save the foster home where they began their lives.
But they'll each need to make a big commitment to the women who run the home to do so!
Find out how in
The Flying Cross Ranch Romances!!!

His Pledge to Protect

His Pledge to Obey

His Pledge to Have

His Pledge to Hold

The Rangers of Purple Heart

The Rancher takes his Convenient Bride

The Rancher takes his Best Friend's Sister

The Rancher takes his Runaway Bride

The Rancher takes his Star Crossed Love

The Rancher takes his Love at First Sight

The Rancher takes his Last Chance at Love

The Brides of Purple Heart

On His Bended Knee

Hand Over His Heart

Offering His Arm

His Permanent Scar

Having His Back

In Over His Head

Always On His Mind

Every Step He Takes

In His Good Hands

Light Up His Life

Strength to Stand

The Rebel Royals series

The King and the Kindergarten Teacher

The Prince and the Pie Maker

The Duke and the DJ

The Marquis and the Magician's Assistant

The Princess and the Principal